MABLE RILEY

A
RELIABLE RECORD
OF
HUMDRUM, PERIL, AND ROMANCE

MARTHE JOCELYN

Tundra Books

Published in Canada by Tundra Books,
75 Sherbourne Street, Toronto, Ontario M5A 2P9

National Library of Canada Cataloguing in Publication

Jocelyn, Marthe
    Mable Riley : a reliable record of humdrum, peril and romance /
Marthe Jocelyn. – Premium ed.

ISBN 13: 978-0-88776-826-2
ISBN 10: 0-88776-826-1

1. Ontario – Social conditions – 20th century – Juvenile fiction.
2. Women's rights – Juvenile fiction.   I. Title.

PS8569.O254M32 2006a   jC813'.54   C2006-904037-0

ONTARIO ARTS COUNCIL
CONSEIL DES ARTS DE L'ONTARIO

We acknowledge the financial support of the Government of Canada
through the Book Publishing Industry Development Program (BPIDP) and
that of the Government of Ontario through the Ontario Media
Development Corporation's Ontario Book Initiative. We further
acknowledge the support of the Canada Council for the Arts and the
Ontario Arts Council for our publishing program.

Printed in Canada

1 2 3 4 5 6   11 10 09 08 07 06

For Mable Rose and Annie Pauline,
my grandmothers
And for Joy and Gordon,
my parents

IDENTIFICATION

Name: Mable Mary Riley

Address: Goodhand Farm, Sellerton, Ontario

Birthdate: April 22, 1887

Hair: I wish I could say raven but really it's dung-beetle brown

Eyes: Blue

IMPORTANT THINGS TO REMEMBER:

SIZES:

Glove: 5   **Pinafore:** Hurrah! Too old for pinafores!

Hat: 21"   **Shoe:** 6½

FAVOURITES:

Colour: Green, the underside of a new leaf

Flower: Forget-me-not

Song: "Bird in a Gilded Cage"

Quotation: "A word is dead / When it is said, / Some say. / I say it just / Begins to live / That day." – Emily Dickinson

Book: Jane Eyre by Charlotte Brontë

Noteworthy Person: Miss Nellie Bly

Wish: To see the world and have the world see me!

FRIDAY, AUGUST 30, 1901

Such a long day of travel we have had before arriving here!
But I may not write about it now, for Viola is scolding me
to blow out the light. She has been such a crosspatch since
we began our journey at 5:30 this morning that I dare not
test her further. How she can think of sleeping, I know not.
I am twitching with excitement, imagining all that awaits
us now that we have left our home. Viola will be quite sorry
that she ordered me to bed, for I shall be wriggling next to
her for several hours yet!

SATURDAY, AUGUST 31
11:45 A.M.

Let me show our new address at once:

> *Misses Viola and Mable Riley*
> *c/o Mr. Howard Goodhand*

Goodhand Farm
Sellerton, Perth County
Ontario, Dominion of Canada
North America
The World

Is this not grand? Viola's new position as teacher in the Sellerton School requires her to board somewhat closer than our crowded little house in Ambler's Corners. After much conversation, it was decided that I should come with her. Hurrah! I had many opinions to contribute, for it was my dearest wish to come away. I quite despair of finding inspiration at home. I do love my dear mother, but she is so weary and dull from her daily toils that her greatest escape is to tell a story to Flossie and Bea at bedtime. I promised to miss my sisters and my brothers, Teddy and Arthur, also, but confess it will be a relief not to be minding them every moment.

In Sellerton I am to take my eighth-grade examinations and be my sister's assistant with the younger scholars. I am determined to keep a record of our adventures this year. Please may there be some!

(We are summoned to luncheon. I will return.)

2:10 P.M.

Luncheon was cold chicken (too dry), buttered peas (a bit slippery), and bread, which was not so light or tasty as Mama's. Mrs. Goodhand has not such a good hand in the kitchen(!).

I had been secretly wishing that after a train journey of such length, we would find ourselves in a new world. Somewhere with mountains, perhaps, and a castle, or a bustling city with bridges and electric lights! I knew better, of course, but there was a small hope to find something extraordinary. Unless the "Station Episode" may qualify? I will recount. . . .

The train brought us to our destination just as twilight wrapped the world in a shimmering cloak of blue velvet. (Am I not poetic?)

Because of the gloom, we could not see much of the town, Stratford, where the station lies. We bid farewell to our carriage companions, a Mrs. Dreyer and her fussy baby. Some partings are a blessing, and we welcomed the sight of the caboose clattering away into the darkening night. We were confused to disembark and discover our party not at hand to meet us as had been promised. It soon unfolded, however, that our host's tardiness allowed us to witness a small drama on the platform.

Another young lady had departed the train with us. She had shining auburn hair and a green cape. She was greeted by a gentleman with a black mustache.

"Helen!" he cried, and flung his arms about her without restraint.

"Oh, Phillip," she said, though how she could breathe to speak, I know not, the embrace being so forceful. I held my own breath, as if it were I who was so entwined.

Next, their noses bumped and then they were kissing, right there on the station platform! Not a brief kiss, either, but lengthy and fueled by passion, I could tell. They were quite heedless of the onlookers, who shortly before had been gathering luggage but now were gaping like yesterday's fish.

I nudged Viola and looked to her to share the thrill of the moment. She was staring quite as hard as I until I caught her eye. "Shush," she said, blushing, and pulled me a little away. Just then a woman with a hefty bosom and a stern look stepped forward to tap the kissing gentleman's arm with the handle of her parasol.

"What are you thinking, man?" she hooted, jabbing him again when he did not break from the embrace. "You must stop this at once! Indecent behaviour is not permitted here!"

The kissers turned to gaze at her, as a cluster of factory girls in smocks giggled from the sidelines.

Sadly, it was at this moment that our driver appeared and beckoned us away. He declared the hovering night an urgent reason to tarry no longer. How I wished to stay and discover more! I shall have to compose more of their story for myself, later.

It was Alfred Goodhand who fetched us. He is the son in the household where the school officers have arranged for us to board. His father, Mr. Howard Goodhand, is away at a barn raising and will not return until Sunday evening. Alfred told us that we may call him Alfred and save the "Mr. Goodhand" for his father.

He is quite a merry soul with a twinkling eye, whom I guess to be about twenty. Without the humorous wink, he might be called lumpen, shaped like a sack of feed as he is. He kept us well amused for the hour it took to drive eight miles from the station. I asked if he knew of a man hereabouts named Phillip, but he did not.

The horse is called Darling. It was Alfred's cousin, Elizabeth, who gave her such a silly name. Her own horse is named Baron, which is much more dignified. I would call my horse Midnight, if ever I had one and she was black.

At the sign announcing our destination, SELLERTON 4 MILES, we spied a figure wobbling along the road atop a bicycle. The rider was hunched over and pedaling fast, cloak flapping like the sail of a toy boat. It was not until we came closer that I realized the cyclist was a woman! Her hair streamed behind her, and she briefly let go of the left handle grip to wave at us.

"Halloo there, ma'am!" Alfred called as we overtook her. I turned to see her grin in the flash of light from the wagon lantern.

"Do you suppose the wind carried off her hat?" asked Viola. "And teased out every hairpin?"

"Oh, that one's not much of a customer for hats," said Alfred, "or hairpins, I shouldn't think."

What did he mean by that? I wondered. I watched her disappear into the dusk, left to ride alone under the stars.

We arrived in the darkness of night. Owls called from unseen perches. Huge black trees, which by morning light turned out to be chestnuts, loomed like giant bat wings over the farmhouse. Alfred unloaded our trunks and the extra box of books – school texts for Viola, novels for me.

Mrs. Goodhand came out to greet us with a lantern. She is a sturdy woman with a plain face. We saw at once where Alfred has inherited his looks. She does not have his twinkle but was kind enough.

SUNDAY, THE FIRST OF SEPTEMBER 1901 –
A NEW MONTH!

We were lazy this morning and did not rise until nearly eight o'clock! We had to hurry to dress, hurry to eat our oatmeal, and hurry to church, not wanting to be late for our first encounter with a new congregation.

I felt a kinship with our Reverend Mr. Farley back home. He was short and round, like a jolly angel, though Methodists do not believe in angels. I've always felt that to be a lack, actually. Surely people would be more faithful if there were pretty paintings of cherubs to contemplate during the boring bits of sermons. Alas.

(When I suggested this to Mama, she said it was yet another indication that I rely too much on appearances and do not pay enough attention to the spirit within.)

The minister at Sellerton Methodist is a Reverend Mr. Scott and has far too many unkempt whiskers to look upon without giggling. Whatever is a man thinking who grows such briars upon his face?

The sermon was "With Faith Shall We Face Our Trials." He spoke well enough but unveiled no mysteries for me. Viola appointed herself my nursemaid and tapped my knee sharply if ever I fidgeted. She seems to think that my behaviour will reflect upon her own standing in the community.

After the service, we shook hands with Mr. Scott. I peered closely at his face to see if some sparrow might be nesting there.

We were joined at the door by Mrs. Goodhand's sister, Mrs. Campbell.

"We're pleased to meet you, Miss Riley," said Mrs. Campbell to Viola. "We live at the next farmhouse along your road. My daughter, Elizabeth, will be one of your Grade-Eight scholars." She pushed forward a pretty girl with honey-coloured hair, who bobbed her head in Viola's direction.

"Oh!" I cried. "You're Alfred's cousin! He told us how you named the horse."

Elizabeth raised an eyebrow. "It's hardly worthy of a squeal," she said, cool as a splash of water.

"You'll find Elizabeth to be a good student, Miss Riley," said her mother, beaming. "She was top speller at the Sellerton School last year. She brought us home a ribbon."

"Isn't that fine," said Viola. "I have decided we'll have spelling bees on Friday afternoons to make for a lively end to the week."

Elizabeth smiled.

"Of course, you'll have some competition from Mable here," Viola continued, "as spelling is the one subject in which she particularly excels."

I cast my eyes modestly down to my boot tips, but not before I saw Elizabeth's irritation eclipse her smile.

More gratifying than that, however, was having Viola declare my cleverness out loud when she normally does nothing but diminish me.

"Does Sellerton please you?" asked Mrs. Campbell.

"Yes, indeed," said Viola, nudging me to answer also.

"We've seen none of it yet but the churchyard," said I. "By next Sunday, I'll know better."

I promptly received a glare from Viola and a squint from Elizabeth.

"Perhaps you do not please Sellerton," she whispered. What had I done to incite such ill humour? Perhaps there is no one hereabouts to contest her cleverness? Or is it simply her nature to be a blot upon the page? I was quite relieved when Mrs. Goodhand remembered the roast and led us away home to the Sunday luncheon.

Mrs. Goodhand may not be the best of cooks, but the servings are abundant. I have yet to see her smile, but she keeps a tidy house without complaint. And wouldn't Mama admire her kitchen! Spacious enough for the table to seat ten if need be. Rows of plates and bowls on the sideboard, not just the one each we have at home.

Mama would find plenty to envy in every room: the fullness of the pillows on the chesterfield; the thick wool blankets stacked at the foot of our bed, awaiting frosty nights; and the width of the porch, which runs right across the front of the farmhouse. Mama has always wanted to sit on a porch at the end of a summer afternoon. The Goodhand farm is a prosperous one. We must be grateful for our good fortune and not dwell on envy.

LATER, SUNDAY NIGHT

We received quite a parade of visitors this evening, the word having got around that the new schoolmistress has arrived. By luck, we overheard Alfred comment that his mother might make an extra pie for later, or Viola and I would have been caught unprepared. Thanks to said remark, however, Viola put on her new collar and I tidied my hair, using my best ribbon. Viola came under much scrutiny from the neighbours, as did her assistant, I'm pleased to say.

Only minutes after the kitchen was recovered from supper, the company began to appear.

"Ah, Mrs. Forrest," said Alfred, opening the door. "I might have known you'd be the first." He went past her into the yard, as though grateful to have animals to tend.

Mrs. Goodhand explained to us that Mrs. Forrest's husband owns the Bright Creek Cheese factory just outside Stratford. I quickly hid my surprise at the sight of her. She was the same woman who had scolded Phillip and Helen for kissing at the train station! She now seemed ready to stand in judgment upon us.

"Well, well, well," said Mrs. Forrest, inspecting Viola as though she were a new dress. Sharp eyes behind spectacles roamed from my sister's hair to her toes. Mrs. Forrest leaned in closely enough to examine Viola's seams.

"We weren't pleased to hear there was a woman hired," she said. "We've never had a woman teaching in these parts."

"I expect there will be more women every year training to be teachers," said Viola. "Times are changing, it seems."

"We're not pleased with the notion of change," said Mrs. Forrest. "Women riding bicycles and such nonsense is more change than we care to entertain. You don't have one of those machines, do you?"

"No." Viola smiled.

"You're very young." Mrs. Forrest sniffed. Perhaps she spoke with regret, as her own bloom was certainly long gone. Her hair was dull, her complexion waxy, her neck a wreath of folds above an unflattering pink shirtwaist with too many flounces. One should not wear flounces upon such an ample form!

"I'm fully nineteen," said Viola, calm and cool. I do admire my sister when she uses that tone on someone other than myself. She turned nineteen three weeks ago.

"I'm trusting two pupils into your care," said Mrs. Forrest, "my precious Cathy and my little Frank. We were most attached to your predecessor, Mr. Tamblyn." She pointed her finger at Viola. "I'll be keeping an eye on you. We expect high standards in these parts."

"I passed my examinations at the Normal School with honours."

"We'll see about honours," said Mrs. Forrest, but first she was seeing about the wedge of apple pie handed over by Mrs. Goodhand.

Next came Mrs. Campbell and Elizabeth, whom I ignored with utmost civility, preferring to help with the tea and pie cutting than to court her snippiness. A while after, a Mr. and Mrs. Brown arrived with their twin boys, Henry and Joseph. I must say, there were never such handsome boys at home! And here is a pair so much alike as two blades of grass!

I saw at once the change in Elizabeth when the boys shuffled into the kitchen. She sparkled like a diamond ring on a lady's finger and used more giggles in ten minutes than in the previous full hour! She is clearly a girl used to being the centre of attention.

"I've been waiting for good company," she complained. "There's no one here worth a moment's conversation."

Viola was engaged with Mrs. Forrest and did not hear Elizabeth continue. "What do you think of our new teacher?"

"She's pretty," said one.

"Ha," said Elizabeth.

I made busy repolishing the teaspoons.

"It's her first appointment," said Elizabeth.

The boys laughed. "Shall we have a dare of who first makes her scream?" They laughed again. That might be a good diversion, I thought. I shall not warn her.

Without appearing to notice them at all, I tried to see which boy was which. I caught them looking my way more than once, so my carelessness was a good plan, I think. No more of them for now. (Except to quickly add that they are black haired, dark eyed, and faintly freckled with a dusting of brown sugar across their identical noses! Oh, lucky me!)

Mr. Goodhand arrived home from his barn raising as the company was leaving, but he was much fatigued and retired directly. We followed shortly, and that was our Sunday.

MONDAY, SEPTEMBER 2, LABOR DAY

Viola says today's holiday was begun in Toronto in 1872, to honour workers and their contribution to society. The towns and cities celebrate with parades and picnics.

Out here in the wilderness, however, Viola and I used the afternoon to finish unpacking. She has taken the top bureau drawers and I must have the bottom.

Alfred carried our trunks to the barn to be stored until we need them to go home next summer. We then took a walk about the farm, acquainting ourselves with the animals and the little forest behind. There are two goats, twenty cows, a bull, a hog, sixteen chickens, three dogs, and a cat named Captain.

The milk from the cows is sold to the Bright Creek Cheese Company. Alfred and his father milk the cows and leave the full cans in a shed by the road, to get picked up and hauled to the factory.

"Good cows make good milk," said Alfred while he showed us around. "Good milk makes good cheese. That's my father's motto. And good cheese feeds the Goodhands!"

Viola looked at me and lifted her eyebrow. I swallowed hard to keep my giggle within.

I now pause in my account to write a letter home. Alfred has offered to take letters to the post office tomorrow, knowing our mother must be eager to hear of our safe delivery here.

It is peculiar to be dropped with a plunk into the heart of another family and to leave our own like old boots in a distant cellar.

LATER

We have learned that it is Mr. Goodhand's habit to sit beside the stove after supper while his wife (and his boarders) clean up the kitchen. He sits in his particular chair, rubbed to threads on the armrests. He selects certain passages to recite aloud from the newspaper and slips in his own comments.

"Will you listen to this," he said tonight.

> **"PERSONAL AND SOCIAL NOTES**
> **The whistle of the Bright Creek Cheese factory, which formerly blew at 6:45 A.M., will in the future blow at 6:40 A.M.**

"That's clever, that is. That's Mr. Francis Forrest who thought that one up. Fourteen employees each coming five minutes earlier gives him more than an hour extra work per day. Figure it out for yourself.

> **"Mr. and Mrs. Abel Davis departed today to spend a week at the Pan-American Exposition in Buffalo.**

"Best of luck to them," said Mr. Goodhand. "Hold your horses – here it is, here it is. We appear to be housing a person of fame under our roof.

"Miss Viola Riley, new teacher of Sellerton School, arrived on Friday and is boarding with Mr. and Mrs. Howard Goodhand, of Goodhand farm.

"Miss Riley was graduated from St. Catherine's Normal School and takes her first position here. She is accompanied by her sister Miss Mable Riley. Although we are saddened by the departure of Mr. Augustus Tamblyn after twenty-eight years of instruction, we wish to welcome Miss Riley to the community."

My first appearance in a newspaper! I shall keep it here as part of my record. Perhaps someday I will perform some further deed of note.

I did my duty and wrote to Mama and to Hattie, also, relating every moment since our arrival. I did not realize how I miss having a friend until I tumbled out my heart to her on paper. It seems many days more than four since waving our handkerchiefs as we drove away.

Our life's adventure began the moment when we faded from their sight, but what did that hour bring for them? Being up so early to say farewell, none of them would have slept enough. Bea was crying and likely Flossie started, too. Teddy would try to be a little man but could not last, I'm certain. Mama was no doubt left with three sobbing children and one big Arthur to fill with oatmeal before he went to the orchard. I hope Mama is not too lonely without us. Perhaps our absence will make her sad again for Father, just when she was becoming used to his being gone.

We have come upstairs now to retire. Viola has decreed that I sleep on the side of the bed under the window. She thinks it a hardship not to sleep above the chamber pot. I do not use the pot in the night, so I shall not suffer. I will wake with chestnut leaves before my eyes and be happy for it.

Tomorrow is the first day of school. If the air is cooler, I'll wear the blue shirtwaist as it advances my eyes. I wonder what the other scholars might be like. Will Henry and Joseph Brown be there? Perhaps there will be a friend for me, since Elizabeth does not seem likely to fill those shoes.

TUESDAY, SEPTEMBER 3 - FIRST DAY OF SCHOOL!

Viola is asleep already, tired from the rigors of her first day of lessons and the responsibility loaded upon her shoulders. I may not keep the light burning too long but must tell a little of our day.

We arose before six to wash and dress, ready to eat with our hosts at half past the hour. I believe that Viola was nervous. She fussed and fumbled so much that it was I who fastened her buttons. As for me, there were bats learning to fly inside my stomach too!

Elizabeth arrived, commanded by her mother to escort us to the schoolhouse.

Alfred was as good-humoured at dawn as he was at dusk, tugging at my braid and calling me "Teacher, miss." Viola snapped at him not to encourage me to think above my place. He turned quite red and stopped at once. "He was teasing, Viola," I said.

"You're to address me as Miss Riley when in the company of your fellow pupils," she said to me, prim and tight mouthed.

"But Alfred is not –"

"Elizabeth is."

"I am more like to call you Bossy Boots," I grumbled.

"Will you begin the day with a detention for disrespect?"

"I think you can make an exception outside the classroom," said Mr. Howard Goodhand, pulling on his boots. "None of us need scolding in our own kitchen."

Now it was Viola's turn to flush, and what pleasure it gave me! I smiled at our host, realizing I had not done so before. He is quite fearsome looking, with eyebrows that might be planted there like a healthy crop of rye across his forehead. His opinions are firmly stated, and they provide the law at the Goodhand farm. (If his wife occasionally disagrees, she is wise enough not to say so in his hearing.)

Viola is accustomed to discussing things with Mama, and she chafes at Mr. Goodhand's "absolute monarchy."

V. and I tidied in silence and put our lunch in pails to bring with us – bread, cheese, and pears provided by Mrs. Goodhand. Elizabeth walked ahead, with her nose sniffing the clouds.

The school is very pretty: gray-painted board and batten, trimmed with black. There are two enormous oak trees in the yard beside. It is quite a new building, perhaps a dozen years old. Before that, school was taught in the church. Viola says she's blessed it's so nice – her friend Carol Anne, from the Normal School, is in a schoolhouse with cracked walls and a leaking roof! Ours has four windows, a good stove, and a little platform at one end for Viola's desk to sit up on.

Miss Riley kept me busy dusting the schoolroom for the arrival of her scholars. The best of my morning duties will be to stand on the top step and ring the brass bell to alert every scholar, cow, and rat within two miles that lessons are beginning.

I was surprised to see my new schoolmates form a line so promptly upon hearing the bell; the previous master must have trained them firmly to make their manners. The boys bowed and the girls each curtsied, from the littlest up to Elizabeth. It was this parade of respect more than anything else, I think, that made Viola believe she is now a teacher!

As soon as all were assembled, we said the Lord's Prayer and then Viola took roll call. There were sixteen scholars today. Only two were missing from the registration list. Viola says we had so many because it is the first day and all the children wanted a peek at her. We will not expect such good attendance during the early autumn months when the farms are still so busy and needing "all hands on deck."

There are four of us in Grade Eight this year: myself, Elizabeth, a Mennonite girl named Adeline, and a boy named Tommy Thomas.

Tommy is a funny boy with big ears and crooked spectacles. He knows the answer to every question posed. Adeline is very sweet and demure, dressed plainly in the custom of the Mennonite people. She will not take the examinations. She says no one in her family has gone to school past the age of fourteen. She will work on the farm and have no more need of book learning. I cannot tell if this makes her sad. If I had no books, I would shrivel up like a dead caterpillar.

The Brown boys alone make up Grade Seven. I had no occasion to speak with them today but have identified their differences. The gap between Henry's front teeth is slightly greater than his brother's. He also has an extra freckle at the corner of his left eye.

There are six long tables for the scholars, placed in three rows. The early grades sit in the front and the older ones at back. The boys sit to the left of the stove and girls on the right. Today I sat with the little ones, though it will depend upon the lesson where I am each hour. Irene is my smallest and cried for her mama all through the morning.

Viola did not drive us hard today. She tried to discover what the pupils had achieved last year in each of the subjects, as she took us through the daily schedule:

Arithmetic
Grammar and Spelling (alternating with Penman-
ship and Recitation)
Geography or Science
Lunch Recess!
Reading and Latin
Drawing, Music, or Sewing to end the day
Except on Fridays: Spelling Bee!

As soon as Viola had announced the routine, an urgent hand shot into the air.

"Cathy Forrest?"

"We are accustomed to arithmetic after lunch, Miss Riley."

"I believe your minds are sharper in the morning," said Miss Riley.

"This will not please my mother," said Cathy Forrest.

"Then she had best not attend Grade Five at Sellerton School," said Miss Riley. "Shall we proceed?"

Ha! I thought. Winning point to Miss Riley.

The trick was played at lunchtime.

We all went outside to eat our lunches in the yard and to catch a last whiff of summer. Miss Riley came with us, though I suspect that Mr. Tamblyn, her predecessor, had never done so.

When she folded back the napkin on her lunch pail, there curled a garter snake, gleaming green against the wedge of cheese. She dropped the pail, and the snake wriggled out across her boots while she struggled not to scream. (Lyddie Thomas and Cathy Forrest, however, squealed loudly enough to wake snakes from here to Toronto.)

The shuffling laughter stopped while we all held our breath. What would she do? (If it were *I* who had put a snake in her lunch, Viola would have yelped and pinched me, but she knew this was a test.)

"There is something you should know about me," said Viola, speaking very slowly and softly, the way our mother does when she is most tried. I think I was the only one to hear the wobble in her voice. The other scholars leaned closer to hear each word.

"This is my first year as a teacher. Last year I was a scholar. I am well aware of all the tricks that scholars like to play. I may be different from Mr. Tamblyn, but being a woman does not mean I will not use a leather strap or the cane. You have been warned." She examined the faces around her, encountering so many blushes and shifting eyes, she could not possibly identify the true culprit(s).

"One other thing," she added. "I am a country girl. Snakes do not alarm me."

Liar, I thought.

"Nor do frogs or beetles or toads. And do not imagine that I will excuse you because it is the first day of school. Since no one cares to accept responsibility, *all* of you will write lines tonight. Now, go and eat your lunch. The bell will ring in twenty-seven minutes."

I was proud of my sister for this speech. She managed to stay calm (though she never does at home) and to give an impression of assurance, whether or not she felt it.

When the afternoon was over, I believe Viola would say her first day was a successful one. She beat a steady rhythm on her desk as the scholars marched out in single file and watched through the window to see the mayhem of release.

I patted her hand. "Well done, Miss Riley."

She smiled, grateful that it was over and she still standing!

THURSDAY, SEPTEMBER 5

Too tired to write. I've had to wash both shirtwaists tonight as well as Viola's, just to be kind, though it did me no good, for she tells me I'm still to check the spelling on all the papers she collected today! And I shall be up early to iron before school.

Mrs. Goodhand is very proud of her new "cool-handle" iron. The handle detaches while the iron is in the fire and thereby stays cool enough to hold with a bare hand! I hope it is not an inconvenience that I will need to heat the iron and use a corner of the table for my board while breakfast is being prepared. Mrs. Goodhand has a disapproving way of folding her lip inside, like pushing a worm back under the earth.

One other thing I must tell – I had my first conversation with Henry Brown. It went like this:

Location: In the little cloakroom behind the classroom. Mable sits upon the bench, tying her boot lace before going into the yard to eat lunch. Henry comes in to fetch forgotten cap.

Henry: Oh!
Mable: Hello.
Henry: Uh. Didn't see you.
Mable: Did I frighten you?
Henry: Uh. No. Didn't see you, that's all.
Henry plucks cap from peg and leaves. Mable leans
head against wall and sighs.

Not a romantic encounter, perhaps, but a beginning.

FRIDAY, SEPTEMBER 6

I have realized in only one week of lessons that to be a teacher is tiring work. There being eight grades at Sellerton, Viola must compose eight lessons for every subject every day. When she teaches the same lesson to two or three grades at once, the results must be graded with different expectations. Her organization is impressive as she plans her roster. If the Grade Threes and Fours are practicing their penmanship, the Grade Fives and Sixes are memorizing Scriptures or poetry and the Grade Sevens and Eights are reciting their passages. Then all must rotate and attend the other tasks. For every grade, history and geography are different lists of dates and battles and kings and lakes and mountains and towns, each to be memorized and recited. Arithmetic is the most complicated of all.

All this labour does not excuse Viola of her ill humour, for she has possessed that always, but it excuses me from lengthy entries in this journal at the end of a school day. I promise to catch things up at the weekend, for this evening I had an assignment to fulfill. Viola requires us (from Grade Five up) to compose a poem about our family. . . .

ODE TO THE RILEY FAMILY

The firstborn is Viola
Known to you as Teacher dear.
You call her Miss,
I call her Sis,
And pray for her good cheer.

Arthur is our steady one,
His mother's helping hand.
He seldom rests,
But often jests
And is a drummer in the band.

How shall I say who I am?
I'm Mable, third in line.

I read, I write,
Dream day and night
Adventure shall be mine. . . .

Flossie is the clumsy one,
She stumbles through her day.
But she is best
At the Hug Contest,
And wins my heart that way.

The six-year-old is Teddy
Though he'd have us call him Ted.
He tries to please
But likes to tease
And fights off going to bed.

And who should be our baby,
Though she is grown past three?
Her face is round,
Her eyes are brown,
She is our merry Bea

Viola need not know I wrote a second verse about her, for it certainly cannot be published:

Viola is a viper
Whene'er she speaks, she stings.
If ever she
Were nice to me
A Heavenly choir would sing!

Ambler's Corners
September 5, 1901

My dear daughters,

How strange that I am writing to you two hundred miles away! That you will read my letter in a room I have never seen, that already you have met people whom your very own mother will never know. Yet how proud I am that you both have the courage to make this true. I'm not certain I would have had the same spirit at your age. Of course, getting married at sixteen and having you, Viola, the following year, changed my dreams from adventure to mothering.

As you encounter a new world, be comforted that life at home has not changed – except that you are not here, my darlings. (I am not yet used to that.) Bea especially does not understand where you have gone. "Where my Maybe?" she asks a dozen times an hour, hunting Mable high and low.

Flossie has taken to sleeping in your bed, thinking herself very brave because of the extra height.

Arthur has begun to pick the back trees, the apples before the pears. He has William Foster to help and a boy from Newtown. Teddy pleaded to work on Saturday and was very pleased with the nickel I paid for his two bushels.

I must patch Teddy's trousers before I pick the peas for supper, so I will sign off for now.

Thank you for writing to tell me how you've settled. I am so proud, as I know your father would be also.

With many kisses,

Your loving mother

Ambler's Corners
September 5, 1901

Dearest Mable,

It comes to me twenty times in a morning that you have moved away. I had only begun getting used to it when your letter arrived and I missed you all over again. How can I bear a whole year apart from you? I implore you not to find another friend while you are gone. All the girls at school are missing you also. Lunch hours are not such fun without you telling stories. I wish you would write some down and send them to me that I may entertain the girls on your behalf.

And it's not only the girls who mourn your absence! Mr. Gilfallen remarked that he would miss your presence because of the blessed quiet in the schoolroom. Jimmy Fender moons about like a lamb who has lost his tail. Naturally, we tease him for this because he gets so very flustered. His ears twitch at every mention of your name.

As for the dashing Brown boys, it seems I am not to trust you to show prudence when a handsome face (or two!) is at hand. Without me at your side to rein you in, your high spirits will perhaps carry you to dangerous places. Please recall yourself on my behalf. And remember that your sister will have no cause for complaint if you are devoted to your studies and other duties.

Our pleasure should come because of our goodness, not in hiding from it.

Please write as soon and as often as you have a penny for postage.

Fondly, your true friend,

Hattie Summers

SATURDAY, SEPTEMBER 7

There is terrible news from the United States. Mrs. Goodhand has been wringing her hands since we heard. President McKinley was shot yesterday while attending the Pan-American Exposition in Buffalo, New York.

The man who did it was an anarchist who gave an assumed name, though it is discovered that his real one is

Leon F. Czolgosz. (There is no instruction in the newspaper as to how that name is pronounced!)

The *Stratford Daily Beacon* declares that the president's wounds may not be fatal. But Mrs. Goodhand says that the particulars of his operation may prove fatal to many a sensitive reader. The newspaper clearly explains how one of the bullets penetrated the abdomen five inches below the left nipple and how a search was made for the exit in the back wall of the stomach, and many other details that are distasteful to dwell on. I find myself reading each account with close attention, as if greater familiarity will alleviate the horror.

Here, it is raining in such torrents that there can be no suggestion of a walk. The cows are hunched together under the trees and seem to be wearing black mud stockings. It is the weather, as well as the poor president, making me feel so dreary, on top of a scolding from Viola and wishing for home.

As crowded as we were in Ambler's Corners, I preferred sharing my room with Flossie and Bea than with Viola, who appears to fancy herself my mother now that we are away. But even our mother left me more to myself, having all the others to mind and mend. V. has only me to bully. My crime to-day was to use her hairbrush! Mine seems to have been abducted by the chestnut tree, for it is nowhere to be found. It cannot be good preparation for a steady demeanor in the classroom that Viola uses hot words over such a small offense. She would be better suited to herding cattle, perhaps, or scaring crows!

Since it still is raining, I shall begin a story to send to Hattie, full of romance and adventure. . . .

A Romantic Novel
~~by Mable Mary Riley~~
~~by Mable Clarabelle Riley~~
by Mable Rosamund Riley

PART THE FIRST
{OUR BOLD HEROINE}

'Twas midnight and the moon shone brightly over the snow, making it appear as though the white mantle of the earth were studded with diamonds.

Away upon the hill we can see an enormous mansion from which brilliant lights are streaming forth. One would think to see the house that an important event was taking place. It was not so, at least not within the earl's knowledge. This old earl, whose wife had long since died, was fond of show, so he always kept his large house lit up with many lights. It is said that it cost him more than $1,000 every year in oil and glass.

He spent much time and money upon his second daughter, indulging her every whim, although she took no notice of it. Helena was the cause of her father's greatest pride and the joy of the whole neighborhood. The people both rich and poor for many miles around looked up to her for help and were seldom disappointed.

Alas! There was a firstborn daughter also, the spiteful ~~Violet Julia~~ Myrtle. This girl was held in no great esteem, for her sour expression and willful temperament were to be avoided rather than sought out. Jealousy of her good sister was made clear in every sharp word and unkind action.

But let us now return to our heroine, for an important event was indeed taking place for her. Allow me to describe Helena.

~~She was not handsome. Her face was plain.~~

By popular judgment she was not perhaps beautiful, but to some she was as lovely as a spring morning. She combed her auburn tresses smoothly back, which showed a full, broad forehead. Her cheeks were rosy red, making almost too great a contrast with the rest of her face, which was white as the snow that blanketed the fields. Her eyes were deep sapphire pools, too thoughtful and bright for common tastes.

Let us watch her now as she treads softly over the wintery terrain. Unbeknownst to Helena, her buttoned boots carry her down a path with many turns and brambles. But for now, her face is lit up, not with the moonlight alone but with the light of love and happiness. Yes, Helena was happy as she ventured out upon the first adventure of her life. For who is that beside her, carrying her case? 'Tis James and he whispers in her ear.

"Oh, my darling, will you return to live under your father's roof, or will you come away with me?"

To be continued . . .

SUNDAY, SEPTEMBER 8
AFTER LUNCHEON

I arrived from the Land of Dreams this morning with a collision, having received Viola's elbow between my shoulder blades. I lay awake wondering why I feel so disheartened until Viola poked me to get dressed for church.

The Reverend Mr. Scott was very earnest this morning. His sermon was "How Will We Be When We Are Old?" I think his intention was to have us study our behaviour and our faith, so that we should grow old with grace. Instead I have been frightened silly that I will live my whole life on a hidden-away farm, ironing my collars and correcting spelling and not ever seeing a big city lit up with electricity or dancing until midnight or being kissed. How will that be when I am old? Having no memories to keep me company while I am waiting for God to take me? Even He will find I am too dull to bother with, and I shall go on living until I waste away to bones from boredom.

I had intended this year in Sellerton to be an adventure! I was to explore unknown places and to experience the unexpected! What has occurred but that I am transported only to another family, with chores and duties and petty arguments, not identical to my own, perhaps, but near enough to be confining. This will not do! It now becomes my purpose to discover an escapade. . . .

AFTER THE TEA BUT BEFORE THE SUPPER . . .

Perhaps it takes only a little determination to change the course of one's life, for here on this very page I declared my yearning for novelty and already have I tripped across it! It came about in this manner: I went to the kitchen earlier, to borrow a needle from Mrs. Goodhand, as mine had jumped into a crack in the floor and hidden there. I heard Elizabeth's cross voice as I entered, and thought at once to leave, but was seen already and could not depart naturally.

"Why must I go?" she complained. "I came only to fetch the soap for my mother. Mrs. Rattle is so peculiar! She speaks recklessly, as if to test me, and she's never grateful in the least for our donations."

"We are being good neighbours," said Mrs. Goodhand, reproving her niece. "I have baked the loaves and they await delivery."

"Why need it be me?" asked Elizabeth as she noticed me in the doorway. "As long as the bread is delivered, why should Mable not be the do-gooder today?"

I was instantly of two minds. I had no wish to perform a task that Elizabeth found distasteful, but I could hear my mother's voice imploring me to "be always quick in doing what is right for others."

"Is there an errand you would have done, Mrs. Goodhand?" I asked, ignoring Elizabeth's smirk of satisfaction. Mrs. Goodhand sighed and wiped her hands upon her apron front.

"There is, Mable, though I do not approve of Elizabeth's reluctance." She explained there is a widow lady of little means, living a mile off toward the town. Mrs. Goodhand makes to her a gift of corn bread every Sunday, though the other women of the church are not so openhanded.

"Because she's mad," said Elizabeth. "Perfectly loony. And she does not go to church."

"Not mad, I think," said Mrs. Goodhand. "But nor is she wholesome."

I felt a shiver climb my spine.

"There is nothing to fear." Mrs. Goodhand saw me flinch and patted my arm. "She will not eat you. That is why you are bringing bread." She used one of her few smiles and sent me to fetch my shawl. I took the bundle and went the way I was pointed, wondering at whom I should find. I expected a withered crone crouching behind brambles, waving a hawthorn cane and muttering dreadful maledictions.

Think, then, of my surprise when the door of a cottage called Silver Lining was opened by a woman only a few years older than Viola, perhaps five and twenty. She wore a most extraordinary ensemble – her skirt coming only to her knees, with wide trousers underneath, gathered tight at the ankles. She wore slippers on her feet coloured the deepest red, as though she'd been wading in blood. She looked like the illustration of a Persian genie in a book, and not at all like a widow lady in a farm cottage in Ontario. It was her dark hair, unconfined and hanging loose about her face, that made me recollect the bicycle rider we had passed on our first night in Sellerton. This must be she!

"Did you think you were arriving at an exhibit, my dear?" she asked, raising one eyebrow high. "Or have you some purpose here other than to stare?"

I closed my mouth, which had gaped without my knowing, and opened it again to stammer, "I am seeking Mrs. Rattle. I am Mable Riley, from the Goodhand farm."

She smiled then and glanced down upon her own self. "They did not warn you that I wore bloomers before they sent you here, Mable Riley?"

"Bloomers, ma'am?"

"My trousers, dear, made popular by Miss Amelia Bloomer and named for her. They are worn by women everywhere who are tired of dragging their skirts across the countryside." She spun about and kicked her legs up with a look of naughty glee. "Are they not clever? I can move whichever way I will!"

They were clever, though most exotic, too. I could see at once why Mrs. Rattle had not joined the fold at Sellerton Methodist.

"I've brought you –" I stopped. This woman did not seem so needful of a neighbour's charity as the one I had imagined.

"Oh! You've brought the Christian bread!" Mrs. Rattle laughed aloud. "Tell me, Mable, are you another relation of Mrs. Goodhand? Like the truculent niece, Elizabeth?"

"No, ma'am. My sister and I are boarding there. My sister is the new schoolteacher, Miss Riley."

"Then I hope it will not offend you to know that my ducks are most partial to Mrs. Goodhand's Holy Loaves?"

"Your ducks, ma'am?"

"When none other of the ladies will even nod in my direction, Mrs. Goodhand is so good as to bake me corn bread every Sunday to perform her charitable duty, is that not right?"

I nodded.

"How cruel, then, to say that her loaves are too dry! They crumble to sawdust and parch the throat. But my ducklings love them and nibble them up in a frenzy!"

She gently pried the bundle from beneath my arm.

"Do come again, Mable Riley," she said, closing the door with a teasing smile.

I was left looking at the little painted sign above the knocker that said SILVER LINING in white script upon a blue background.

Now I must devise a way to visit her again, without allowing Elizabeth to know that I desire it, else she might thwart me. Common sense tells me that Mrs. Rattle is not a godly woman, or even an admirable one. And yet I am drawn to her as to no one else in Sellerton. Already I have smiled too often at her use of "truculent" when describing Elizabeth. Does this mean I am weak and easily corrupted? I feel I have eaten a cake all to myself and must have yet another taste!

THURSDAY, SEPTEMBER 12, PAST 10:00 P.M.

Why has it fallen to me, I wonder, to soak the vegetable garden, feed the chickens, and scrape Mr. Goodhand's boots each evening? Nonetheless, I did all my chores quickly so that I might study for tomorrow's spelling bee. I am determined to oust Elizabeth from first place!

Shortly after supper, I went to "Endeavour" with Viola, Elizabeth, and Alfred. It is the custom hereabouts to visit the church on Thursday evenings for an extra lesson and choir practice. Viola is in the choir, as is expected of the teacher. I do not sing. My sister says I am no asset to a choir, unless it were composed of frogs! Alfred, however, is revealed to have a melodious baritone voice.

During the walk home, as the evening advanced to darkness, he and Viola continued to rehearse the hymns learned at Endeavour. Elizabeth and I dallied behind, not wishing such a serenade. It was the first occasion of our being alone together, and one might guess I did not take pleasure in it. On the contrary, for I wished to question her on the subject of Mrs. Rattle.

"Where has she lived before now?" I asked. "Or did she always live hereabouts?"

"She moved into that cottage only in June. They say she may have lived in the United States or some say France."

"And what of Mr. Rattle? Is he long dead?"

"She has never mentioned him," said Elizabeth. "I confess I have wondered that myself. My mother says no widow who loved her husband could wear such nonsense."

"Perhaps he traveled to the Klondike River in search of gold and froze to death on a mountain pass, leaving her with no support. Or perhaps he died while away in Africa, fighting the Boers? And was honoured with a medal! Or was gravely ill and nursed to the end by her tenderness? Or was murdered, perhaps, by a jealous lover in a fit of unharnessed desire!"

Elizabeth stopped on the spot and stared at me with such a look as to bring my imagination to a halt.

"Only that she is peculiar," I mumbled, "as you said yourself. One would not expect a person such as she in a place such as this."

"No, indeed," said Elizabeth. "Nor will she be present for long, if Mrs. Forrest has anything to do with it."

"Has she offended in some way?"

"She has . . . opinions." Elizabeth's voice dropped to a whisper. "And does not withhold them." Crickets chirruped at the side of the path, and "Rock of Ages" wafted back from Viola and Alfred far ahead.

Opinions. The very word, when spoken in this way, was chilling to the bone, as though it were some dread disease and Mrs. Rattle too far gone for salvation. I said no more and hurried up my pace.

FRIDAY, SEPTEMBER 13

Grrr! Viola has had one of her dismal ideas. We are to have two teams for the spelling bee each Friday so that we must depend on one another to win! My own ability becomes irrelevant! It is my good fortune to have Tommy instead of Adeline, who stumbles dreadfully. However, I have Cathy Forrest, who seems to misspell intentionally so that she might weep explosively for all to pity her. I am also blighted with the near-idiot Dottie Blau, in Grade Three. I will be drilling the younger ones endlessly if we're to have any hope of winning. To-day was only a demonstration match, but it still is sad to record that we did not have the superior score. Thankfully, it does not count toward the total.

The worst part is that Viola has assigned us *names!* I am captain of the Cheerful Commas and Elizabeth is captain of the Happy Hyphens! Grrr! Why not the Addled Apostrophes? Or the Quacking Mad Quotation Marks???

For the first mile of the walk home, I wheedled and coaxed as best I could that Viola might change the plan. She ignored my pleas, and for the second mile I refused to speak to her. But then we came home to such a fuss that I must feel sorry for her again!

Upon our arrival, Mrs. Goodhand was serving tea to Mrs. Forrest on the veranda. As Mrs. Goodhand is not the sort of woman to entertain in the middle of a workday, we knew as we approached there was a serious matter at hand.

"I hope no one has died," said Viola.

It soon became clear that *we* were the object of the visit, for Mrs. Forrest pushed her teacup aside, leaving it tipped in her hurry, and struggled to her feet, very red of face. Mrs. Goodhand made an effort to soothe her, but we were on the porch steps by now and the fuss had begun.

"I'm surprised you'd have them in the house, Hazel," said Mrs. Forrest, pinning Viola with a fiery eye. "You may be overcharitable with certain women, but I've never known you to have time for downright hussies, particularly where your Alfred is involved."

"Now, Suzanna," said Mrs. Goodhand.

My thoughts seized upon Mrs. Forrest's name being Suzanna and far too pretty for her, but she was speaking again and jabbing her finger in Viola's direction.

"It is my daily obligation to set a fine example for my precious Cathy. Is it right that I should send her off to be instructed by a mere girl, with morals so loose they're falling out like old teeth?"

"Now, now, these are good girls. It must be a misunderstanding."

"What is the trouble?" asked Viola. "What is it you think I've done?"

"Think? As if I didn't hear it with my own two ears!"

"What, Mrs. Forrest? What did you hear?"

"I heard singing! Don't you deny it! As I traveled home from the church last night! God's own hymns being la-de-dahed like common music hall songs. And she wasn't alone, Hazel! That's the worst of it. She was accompanied by your son, Alfred, whose voice I would recognize anywhere. I'd not have believed it of him, but hussies like her take pleasure in leading good boys astray. Did you know they were out together? In the dark?"

She swayed a little in her temper and sat with a thump into her chair, fanning her neck with a limp glove. Why did Viola not defend herself but instead hold her breath?

"Your accusations are ridiculous," I said, tapping my foot on the step in my impatience.

"Mable!" Viola's hand reached out to hush me, but I kept on.

"They weren't alone! We all walked home together from Endeavor! Elizabeth and I were only a few steps behind. Surely God is as pleased to hear Viola singing under the open heavens as He is in a church. It was lovely, like a ghost chorus."

Mrs. Forrest glowered at Mrs. Goodhand, as if she were responsible in some way. "How do you tolerate this insolence?"

Mrs. Goodhand seemed to make up her mind about something. She waved her hand at Viola and me, to shoo us away. We shuffled toward the kitchen door but did not enter.

"I will speak to Alfred," she said to Mrs. Forrest. "I will hear the whole story from every person. There is no need for you to be overly heated on the matter, Suzanna. I perceive no harm to Cathy yet."

"Am I to wait until the harm is done, then?" Mrs. Forrest stood up again, glaring at Viola as her hands clawed at the table for support. "You may be certain that I am ever vigilant. You are being watched at every brazen turn."

"I shall keep it in mind, Mrs. Forrest," replied Viola, admirably without a breath of impudence. "I thank you for instructing us as to local custom." She swept into the house, leaving me to hear Mrs. Forrest erupt anew.

"Local custom? When is moral behaviour a matter of local custom?"

Mrs. Goodhand accompanied the visitor through the gate.

We shelled the peas without a word passing between us. Viola's cheeks were quite pale until bedtime, when washing brought the colour back. It was not until then that I dared to ask her why she'd held her tongue so firmly.

"It will do no one a lick of good if I lose my place," she said quietly. "The children need a teacher and Mama needs my salary."

"What about you, Viola? What do you need? Is it not tempting to tell that nosy old bat what a horror her 'precious' Cathy is already?"

"Temptation is put before us in order to be overcome," she replied in her most prim and aggravating voice.

She made one remark further, as we pulled up the eiderdown: "If a girl's reputation is so fragile as this, what must it be like for a woman who has truly fallen?"

My dearest Mable,

Your story has been the saviour of our lunch hours this week and kept us guessing all manner of outcomes! Please send another chapter at once! We have been suffering inclement weather, so our meals at school are taken indoors, making your entertainment even more welcome. I worry, however, that it is so wicked. Please make Helena repent.

Lindsey says your brother Arthur is paying his attentions to her sister, Laura. Do you know the truth of that? He has had a haircut that shows white spots on either jaw where the sun had not touched! He may want to wait a few days before calling on Laura Melbourne until his sideburns have grown a little! It is daring enough that he thinks a banker's daughter will love a fruit farmer's son, let alone one with a labourer's sunburn!

We are beginning algebra. Mr. Gilfallen has no patience for idleness or diversion (as you well know!) and pinned Bonnie's braid to the wall when she did not provide the correct answer. But how could she? We've only just begun the algebraic theories! Is your sister teaching you the same? I wonder if you will be behind us or ahead when it comes time for the examinations?

Jimmy Fender asked if I knew of your address. I said I would discover if you would like to receive a letter from him. (Or are the handsome Browns still too distracting by far?)

With fond wishes,

Your friend,

Hattie Summers

PART THE SECOND
{A TOO HASTY DEPARTURE}

James's breath upon Helena's ear tickled as he whispered to her. "Will you come with me, Beloved?"

"If I go with you, I succumb to the temptations I have always sought to resist," she cried.

"Yes, my dear," he said, "but truly 'tis past time to suffer a change of heart. Your father will wonder already not to see you by his left hand at supper."

So on they sped, leaving their tracks in the velvety snow as a traveler on the desert sands. The nearest railway station was about a mile. To this they hastily went, with Helena clutching her portmanteau full of jewels and some moneys for fare and other necessary expenses.

Did it not occur to our heroine to wonder why

'twas she who paid out the money? No, indeed, not yet, for still she looked upon James's bright eyes and twirling mustache with great affection.

As the train pulled away from the station, Helena spied Mr. Edwards, the stationmaster, waving his handkerchief in farewell. He was a man she had known since childhood, always with a kind word and a striped peppermint. Helena felt a tearing in her heart as she left all she knew and loved behind her. Such scenes, once imprinted upon our memories, will not so easily be erased. Helena spent a very wakeful night.

James, however, was dreaming of the future that he hoped to have. As we shall see, James's purpose for carrying Helena from her father's arms was a double one. Let us watch him. He is not the man he appears.

As the night grew deeper, Mr. Edwards also was unable to set his mind at rest, for he had witnessed Helena's companion and was not pleased. Though his opinion of the earl's other daughter was a low one, he resolved to speak with her on the morrow.

To be continued . . .

SUNDAY, SEPTEMBER 15

I did not hear a word of the sermon this morning, except to know its title, "How Best to Secure Our Place in Heaven." I am certain it was edifying, but I had my mind taken with other things, such as Mrs. Rattle and how best to secure a visit there to-day.

I need not have worried, for Mrs. Goodhand spoke with me as we came home from the service, asking if I would like to be the messenger again. I hastily agreed to do the errand. Two o'clock found me standing on the doorstep of Silver Lining cottage.

Mrs. Rattle was dressed again in her "bloomers," with a shirtwaist of scarlet, giving the impression of a British soldier at ease. When she answered my knock, I held out the bundle from Mrs. Goodhand.

"Will you come in to-day, Mable Riley?" she asked, taking the loaf.

"I had better not," I said. I felt that Mrs. Goodhand would not approve of me carrying her charity past the door. But perhaps she could not complain if I helped put it to use under God's own sky? "May I see your ducks instead?"

Mrs. Rattle knew at once my thinking, for she laughed a hearty laugh and led me behind the cottage, where she has built a little duck pen using dead tree branches knit together to form a "briar patch" fence. There is a small pond at the bottom of a grassy incline, and the ducks paddled about most contentedly.

Mrs. Rattle made a queer clucking noise in her throat and was soon surrounded by her flock. I helped to unwrap Mrs. Goodhand's corn loaf, and it crumbled immediately into duck-sized morsels. What a party they had, pecking and quacking and edging one another out of the way with their floppy feet.

I was sorry when they had finished their share, for it meant my visit was over for to-day. Mrs. Rattle escorted me back to the road, speaking only to admire the maple trees, beginning to dress themselves in their autumn golds.

"The name of your cottage is a pretty one," I said before taking my leave. "How did you think of it?"

Mrs. Rattle tilted her head and began to recite in a low voice.

"Was I deceiv'd, or did a sable cloud
Turn forth her silver lining on the night?

"It is by John Milton," she said, "From *Comus,* an epic poem."

"What does it mean, exactly?" I asked.

"To me it means that my little cottage is a spot of brightness in a dark world," she said, looking away over the rolling meadow.

I hovered for a moment between good manners and curiosity.

"Is the world so very dark?" I asked.

Her eyes came back to rest on mine, gray like a rainy pond.

"I have often wondered whether children should be warned of what lies ahead," she said. "Girls, in particular, are forced to don a heavy harness without much preparation."

Aha! I thought. One of her opinions! I recollected Elizabeth's hushed voice.

"Would it be better to arrive on the doorstep of womanhood trained to do battle? Or should children remain unfettered so long as they are able?"

"I don't know," I stammered as she seemed to pause for a reply. "I'm not sure I understand what we should be fighting for?"

"You will be fighting to be heard, Mable Riley." Her voice lifted. "You will be fighting for the right to vote, as men do. You will be fighting to end injustice against women in the workplace. You will be fighting for a voice!"

She raised a fist and clicked her heels and gave me a triumphant salute before closing the door of her cottage. I felt a giggle rising in my throat and ran like a rabbit down the road before my laughter could escape me.

MONDAY, SEPTEMBER 16

The news from the United States is sad. President McKinley died on Saturday, the strain upon his heart too much to pursue recovery.

Vice President Theodore Roosevelt has hurried back from his holiday to become the twenty-sixth president of the United States of America. Sir Wilfrid Laurier, our Canadian prime minister, said he "received the news with keen regret."

Even the king sent a telegram:

MOST TRULY DO I SYMPATHISE WITH YOU AND THE WHOLE AMERICAN NATION AT THE LOSS OF YOUR DISTINGUISHED AND EVER TO BE REGRETTED PRESIDENT.

EDWARD REX

The newspaper reports that Mrs. McKinley is bearing up well, but whatever does that mean? If she truly loved him, she must be distraught beyond measure. When I am married, I hope I will not "bear up well" if a ruthless killer shoots my husband. I hope to love so deeply that I will tear out the hair from my head and hurl myself at walls to distract from the pain within.

Did Mama not cry every night, with the quilt pulled high to muffle the sound? Though by day, it's true, she bore up well. There was too much work to be done and babies to care for.

It makes me wonder again about Mrs. Rattle's loss. Did she love her husband? As she never mentions him, does this mean she is bearing up well? Or has she gone mad with grief? Her proclamations about battling women could be a symptom of her affliction. I am determined to discover the truth.

TUESDAY, SEPTEMBER 17

I have not told Viola what I learned of Mrs. Rattle's convictions. Whether this is because she might sneer or that she might forbid me to visit again, I am not certain.

I find I look forward to Mr. Goodhand's comments upon the news in the *Stratford Daily Beacon*. I am discovering that hearing another's convictions on a subject helps to form one's own, whether in agreement or in opposition.

"PERSONAL AND SOCIAL NOTES"

he read this evening.

"Bright Creek Cheese factory is hiring more labour for the busy autumn season. Applicants should inquire to Mr. Francis Forrest, manager.

"Humph," said Mr. Goodhand. "His profits are increasing while his milk order stays the same?

"Joseph Power, the capable and obliging milk hauler, has completed his contract this fall. His many friends hope to see him on the route next summer.

"If he can manage to stay out of the whiskey on the evening run, we'll be happy enough to see him.

"A meeting of the Ladies Reading Circle will take place on Sunday afternoon at the home of Miss Thyra Robertson. All ladies are welcome. Sandwiches will be served.

"Bad enough to waste time reading a book," said Mr. Goodhand. "Let alone having tea parties to waste more time talking about it."

WEDNESDAY, SEPTEMBER 18

When I open the reading primer each afternoon, I shudder with dread. We spend an hour in dreary woe, listening to one child after another read from the *Saunders' New Ontario School Reader*, book 1:

"Ann may sell a bun.
Sue may buy a bun.

Dick may sell a gun.
Tom may buy a gun.

Sal may sell a cake.
Lil may buy a cake.

Nick may sell a rake.
Nell may buy a rake."

And so on . . . The lessons have been written as a sleeping spell. More than once I have given Peter or Ellen a jiggle to wake them up. Viola is most impatient when she hears their efforts to read aloud.

I feel very sorry for little Peter Rubens, Adeline's younger brother. His right arm is broken and bandaged from a fall. "Off the barn roof," he says, though he is only just seven and I wonder that he would be allowed to climb so high.

Frank is the son of Viola's foe, Mrs. Forrest, and brother to Cathy. Frank will not stop scratching, and I am quite sure he is flea infested. He claims to sleep with two dogs upon his bed. One of the dogs must sleep across his head, to muffle his father's snoring.

My girls are Ellen and Irene. If only Ellen could keep her finger from her nose, she would be a great deal more appealing. Irene has finally stopped crying for her mama every morning and now cries when it is time for dismissal instead. She has the fairest skin – forever smeared with ink, however I try. Her mother has written a letter to Viola requesting that Irene be permitted to use only a pencil.

Ambler's Corners
September 17, 1901

My dearest Mable,
Your second letter came upon the tail of the first and was considerably entertaining. How I chuckled over your

encounter with the mad suffragist Mrs. Rattle! Oh, that I had been with you to roll our eyes and egg her on! We might have drawn yet more lunacy from her and had "opinions" to divert us for many a day. You must discover more about her mysterious past and vanished husband. Does she seem to you like a murderess?

As for poor Helena's plight, it is quite as difficult to await the fictional outcome as the true! Write another chapter at once!

I have a small romance to report at this end, and it involves a person near and dear to you. Have you guessed? Your brother Arthur is seen *every* evening visiting Laura Melbourne, sitting on her veranda, or once even taking in laundry from the clothesline when it began to rain all of a sudden! Very intimate, think you not?

School is much the same as it always was, except that you are not here, chattering in my ear and driving Mr. Gilfallen to distraction. We had our first arithmetic quiz to-day. I missed only one question that I know of. You, most probably, would have had a perfect score. The one good thing about your absence is that I will have the opportunity to stand first upon occasion.

Bonnie and Stella are in dreadful trouble for using playing cards in the yard. You know how Mr. Gilfallen disapproves of gambling. We have yet to hear of their punishment. I know not what to think of the matter. I wish I could hear your opinion.

That's all for tonight, my dear friend.

Affectionately,

Hattie Summers

THURSDAY, SEPTEMBER 19

I have been thinking that 1901 is a sad year for the world, with two great leaders having died.

First, Queen Victoria, in January. Mrs. Goodhand has kept a scrapbook since she was a young girl, presenting every notice and picture she ever found of the queen, including many of the funeral. Of course, Victoria was very old. I suppose with eighty-two years' worth of accomplishments, her thoughts will be occupied for eternity in Heaven. If one has not lived a full life, one might waste time in Heaven regretting the brevity of one's earthly hours, which is not what Heaven is for.

President McKinley will be busy in Heaven trying to forgive his assassin and perhaps praying for his wife to bear up well. Something I am curious about is this: Once a person is in Heaven, does he indeed watch over his family and other worldly acquaintances? As one might watch a village street through the parlour window? And are there shutters to open and close?

I ponder this because I wonder how my father passes his days in Heaven. Does he know we miss him? Does he look upon us wistfully, also knowing (dare I say it?) that we miss him less as the months and years go by? There are times when I wish that my father could be witness to my life. When I recite well at school or finish my chores and help the little ones finish theirs.

More often, however (and I write this in very small letters that no one should ever read it), I admit that I should be mortified or ashamed to think that my every action is on display. I am not wicked or lazy, but I do not want my father (or my mother or Viola or any other person) to see me as I travel through my day.

For instance, on the subject of boys . . . How greatly it would affect me to imagine my own father watching every encounter! Both Brown boys spoke to me to-day, one after the other. If it does not sound too vain, I venture that they had between them a dare to do so!

Joseph caught me first, as I walked back to the class-room after eating my apples and cheese. His step fell in with mine and he grinned at me sideways before checking over his shoulder where his brother stood with Tommy

Thomas. I pretended not to note that we had an audience and tossed my braid most charmingly.

"Hey," said Joseph.

"Hey, yourself," said I. "Am I a horse and wanting hay?"

"Uh, no," said he, then took a great swallow as if to make himself more brave. "I am to say . . . I mean . . . I was to ask you . . . I mean . . ." He glanced around once more. "Could you just nod," he whispered, "and not mind that there's no question spoke aloud?"

We were by now at the door, and I stopped with my foot upon the lowest step.

"No," I said, shaking my head, "I cannot agree without knowing why." As soon as my head did move, the hoots began from the watching boys. I smiled at Joseph's fallen face, to give him courage for the next attempt.

It was after lessons that Henry found me sweeping the classroom while Viola closed the shutters from without.

"Mable?" he said.

"Well, at least you have learned my name," said I. "Your brother addressed me 'Hey!'"

"Was that the reason you refused him?"

"I was asked nothing to refuse," said I.

Viola choosing that moment to appear, I bent to my sweeping most industriously. (Would I have acted differently if I knew my father were watching me from his porch chair in Heaven?)

"Do you need a task, Henry Brown?" asked my sister.

"No, ma'am."

"Do you keep your hat on to speak with your teacher?"

"No, ma'am." He slid it off.

"Have you somewhere to be?"

"Yes, ma'am." And away he went.

Viola did not scold me as I expected and was quite pleasant as we began our journey homeward.

"Viola?"

"Mmmm?" Her thoughts were elsewhere, on Tennyson, perhaps, or the fifth years' inability to repeat their times tables.

"Viola, is teaching what you thought it would be?" I asked. "Or does the tedium of discipline outweigh the satisfaction of instruction?"

She gave me her attention now but did not yet answer.

"There seems to be so little satisfaction," I added, laughing. "Hearing Cathy Forrest recite *The Fairy Garden* can scarcely be why you chose to become a teacher!"

"There is no choice, Mable," said Viola. "You will be a teacher too, until you marry. That's what girls do. Our mother needs our help and so we teach."

"It seems to suit you," I ventured, not adding that

bossing a whole roomful of children must multiply the pleasure of bossing a sister.

"I like it more than I imagined," she said. "And perhaps that makes me better at it than I expected. I was afraid I would stand before you all with a mouth full of cotton, unable to speak. But lessons seem to move along quite smoothly, do they not? I find success lies in the planning."

We walked along in silence for a bit, until I thought of something else to say. "I like the part of teaching when I see upon their faces the light of understanding. But it does not occur so very often. I think I would rather do something else when it comes time. Perhaps I could write novels. Or better yet, I'll be an adventurer and travel to France or Africa!"

"There's no one going to pay you for your silly stories, Mable," said Viola sharply. "And certainly no earnings to be had exploring the Nile River. If your geography grades are any indication, you will not find your way out of Perth County."

And with that, she marched ahead at a determined pace.

I loitered behind, collecting pinecones from the roadside, knowing that Mrs. Goodhand likes to use them for scrubbing her pots. I had quite a lovely wander by myself, and heard a bobolink call out its evening song.

FRIDAY, SEPTEMBER 20

The reading lessons have continued to vex me considerably, but to-day I discovered a remedy.

It drives me to distraction hearing Frank Forrest pause for several seconds before each word and then read like a whining wasp. The texts were no doubt written by the most pious and well meaning of instructors, but they make for tedious reading. I remember them well from my own primary days and was tired of them then!

> "As we have two ears and but one tongue, we should hear much more than we speak."

That word *tongue* holds such a trick that none of the children can grasp it.

I looked at the clock above Viola's desk when Frank began his turn to-day and counted four minutes and a half for him to read this poem, with grubby fingers scratching at his flea-bitten ankles in accompaniment.

> "Our ears were made to hear.
> Our tongues were made to talk.
> Our eyes were made to see.
> Our feet were made to walk."

It was no surprise to find Peter's eyelids flopping down like window shades at noon. Seized with inspiration, I took up my slate and wrote upon it my own poem, using words from Lesson 3.

"Here, Ellen," I said, passing the slate to her. She is the best reader of the four and began without hesitation.

"One flea I see by my left eye.
One flea is sat upon my knee.
One flea is near my ear, I fear.
The fleas on me add up to three!"

The children began to giggle without restraint. Viola was swift to wonder what could cause such merriment during a reading lesson. I begged the children to take their turns quietly, feeling that my rhyme should remain our little secret.

My satisfaction dissolved, however, when the spelling bee took place.

I made no error. Tommy made no error. Even Ellen and Peter made no error. It was Cathy Forrest, spelling *poured* without the *u* or the *e* and Dottie, who started *copper* with a *k*, who helped the Happy Hyphens win again. They have accrued thirty-two points to our twenty-four. This is dismal!

Part the Third
{The Train Journey}

For Helena and James, the journey continued. Unable to rest, Helena found her gaze wandering to the carriage window with the black of midnight behind, reflecting nearly as clear a picture of herself as if it were the gilt-framed mirror in her bedchamber at the earl's mansion.

It showed her pale face, worry-smudged eyes, and rosy lips. It also showed her traveling cloak of green velvet trimmed with white rabbit fur and, faintly, the glinting of a brooch pinned above her heart.

But Helena had no patience to examine her own reflection and peered into the darkness beyond, pondering the lives lived in these farms and towns away from her own familiar valley.

Chugging through a village, Helena espied a small house with a candle burning in an upstairs window. Despite the lateness of the hour, the shadow of a woman was clearly outlined through the curtain.

Oh! thought Helena. *There stands a house disturbed by sorrow this night!* Her tender heart wondered what caused a light to flicker near to dawn. Perhaps the woman cries to have lost her loving sister, not to illness or insanity but worse even than that! Lost to an immoral misstep, abandoned by a thoughtless, selfish act whose consequences will rain down more heavily than tears!

"No!" Helena stumbled to her feet but fell back at once, flung by the motion of the train into her seat beside James, the slumbering scoundrel.

"I have acted in haste!" she cried, looking upon James's features, which were abhorrent to her now. "Can it be too late to be forgiven?" She reached out a hand to wake him, to confess the strain upon her heart, but at that moment felt the train struggle to make an unexpected stop. Shouts of confusion, ladies screaming, and gunshots combined to produce a most alarming clamour. James came awake at last, his lips making a noisy smacking sound.

"What is the matter?" he called most unmanfully, not hiding the fear in his voice.

"I cannot tell for certain," replied Helena. "But it would appear that this train has been apprehended by bandits!"

To be continued . . .

Mrs. Forrest made an announcement after the service this morning. The Harvest Social will be held in the cellar hall of the church on Saturday night, October 26. From the very youngest girls up to those who might have an eye to courting, there was much excitement and fluttering, mostly on the subject of which dresses will be worn and which of the young men will deign to attend.

The sermon was "God Is Best Worshiped in His Own Home." I think perhaps that Mrs. Forrest and the Reverend Mr. Scott have discussed the topic. He was insistent that church is the place for hymns and prayers; otherwise they may go misdirected and not to God's heart. No, thought I, but fly instead to the fleshy ears of a busybody down the lane.

The sermon seemed three hours long and lunch quite the same, so eager was I to see Mrs. Rattle once more. When I finally arrived at Silver Lining, I knew not what to expect. What I discovered was Mrs. Rattle, standing beside her shed, swinging an ax.

"Aha!" she cried. "Just the person I need! You've probably seen this done before, have you not?"

Mrs. Rattle felt warned, she said, by the temperature dipping these past few nights and had decided to chop a supply of firewood in preparation for winter. However, she explained, she is a city girl and knew not how to begin.

"Could you not hire someone?" I asked. "This is a man's chore, surely."

Her face shadowed and she turned to me quite sharply. "There should be no such thing as a man's chore, Mable Riley. If women are so reliant upon men, even to the fire beneath their teakettles, how are we ever to speak out using our own voices?"

This seemed an answer beyond the question, but I saw that she was determined to do the work herself.

"Allow me to show you how to hold the ax," I said. From watching my brother a thousand hours I knew that much, at least. I needed also to set up her chopping block, for she had the large piece lying on the ground at an awkward angle.

"Freddy Abell at the blacksmith's delivered this to me," she said, indicating the pile of wood that blocked the entrance to the shed. "I was wondering aloud where I might find some, and he said I could have a tree that fell on his lot last year. I have quite used up the supply that was put here by the owner of the cottage when I moved in."

She sighed and then grinned. Her smile makes me think of a clever cat. She prodded a log with the toe of her boot (which was green and laced to the top with silk ribbons). "It is quite dry enough to split, Freddy said. But

I did not think the pieces would come so large. They need to fit into the stove.

"That Freddy Abell thinks he has earned a place in Heaven for helping me. Usually men assume I am a demented suffragist for wearing bloomers, or else yearning for a husband. Trust me, that is the furthest wish from my heart!"

Whatever does that mean? I wonder.

As much as she wished to appear self-sufficient, she did look a helpless lamb in the face of such a woodpile. She was a quick learner, however, handling the ax as I instructed and even grunting faintly with each swing. We became so absorbed that many minutes passed before she spoke again.

"Tell me, Mable Riley, what are your dreams?"

I jumped, as if she were tickling me with a feather.

"I – well – I – I suppose I will be a teacher," I stammered. "Until I marry, of course."

"Marry? Surely it is too soon to think of marrying?" She tipped her head to one side and beamed her gray eyes straight at me. "What about a little deeper, hmmm? In your heart, Mable? What do you wish for?"

Mrs. Rattle does not conform to the usual code of manners, and yet she cannot truly be called rude. She steps over the threshold and into the parlour without awaiting an invitation. But she seems to know already that her company is welcome.

I told her what I have not told to anyone (except Viola, and only then to hear the words spoken aloud. I could rely on her not believing in me).

"I want to be a writer," I whispered.

She smiled the most beautiful smile. "I knew when I first saw you that we would like each other," she said. "I am a writer too."

"You are? Have you been –?"

"Published? Yes, my dear. But not books. I write for newspapers." A shadow fell across her face. "Or rather, I *did* write for newspapers until I began too often to write the truth. Now, I am . . . well . . . considering what may next be suitable for me."

"You wrote for newspapers? You were a reporter? Like Nellie Bly?"

Mrs. Rattle laughed. "Why, yes! Nellie Bly is a heroine to me. Her life is partly why I chose mine."

"Nellie Bly went on her voyage around the world during the year that I was two," I told her, "in 1889. When I was a little girl, Viola and Arthur used to load my cradle with provisions and then climb in with me and rock it wildly until we nearly tipped into the shark-infested ocean. They called it Playing Nellie Bly. It was our best game, all squeezed in and laughing till our breath was ragged."

"That's a lovely memory!" she said. "There was only me at home. I always wished for sisters."

"Sisters are not always so lovely," I said.

It was not until our hands were rubbed sore and our faces moist with perspiration that Mrs. Rattle decided we had done enough for one afternoon and said to please come inside for a glass of lemonade.

It would take half the night to tell of the wonders inside Silver Lining. As soon as I stepped in the front door, I felt a rush of excitement from my scalp to my toes and knew not which way to look first.

"Come into the kitchen," she said, leading me too quickly through a large parlour, where I saw a dancing woman wearing only a gauzy scarf, painted directly on the wall. I must have gasped aloud, for she laughed.

"Whatever would Mrs. Forrest have to say about my hobby, hmmm?"

My face grew hot. It was exactly what I had been thinking! I don't suppose I expected a tidy sofa like Mrs. Goodhand's or a plain kitchen like my mother's, but nothing could have prepared me for these rooms!

The kitchen was painted pink like the inside of a new

peony. Her pretty crockery I recognized from the T. Eaton Company catalogue. It has pink-and-green decoration, set with heavy gold lines – the king cannot have nicer, I am certain.

She opened her icebox and chipped chunks of ice off the block with an awl kept handy on a leather cord. She put the chips into crystal glasses, which she filled with lemonade, already prepared and cooled. Never did a drink quench my thirst so deliciously!

When we returned to the parlour, I forced my eyes to see beyond the naked dancer to the other furnishings. The chairs and occasional tables were all made of wicker, covered with cushions of many lush brocades. There were shelves from the floor to ceiling along one wall, filled with books. There were framed photographs and pictures hanging from the other walls and small toys and figurines standing on every surface.

Except for one. What did I spy upon the desk?

"A typewriting machine!" I cried. "That's what it is, am I right?" I touched one of the letter keys with the tip of my fingernail.

"It will not bite you," she said, laughing. Though she appears quite melancholy in her quiet moments, she seems always to be laughing when she speaks – a warm, gentle laugh, as though every thought amuses her.

"This is my friend Underwood," she said with a look of pride. "Underwood, this is Mable Riley. I hope you may become better acquainted." Mrs. Rattle plucked a piece of paper from the stack on the desktop and rolled it, with a flourish, into the machine.

"Underwood, say hello to Mable." She hit several keys firmly with the pads of her fingers. Her nails were torn and dirty from our afternoon in the woodpile. She pulled the paper out and showed me the words she had typed: *Hello, Mable.*

"Hello, Underwood," I said aloud, grateful that Hattie was not there to hear me.

"I pray that I will not have to sell this," said Mrs. Rattle. "I will let almost anything else go first."

I did not like to hear such a remark. We've been taught that a lady does not discuss money. But I had to know.

"You don't seem poor," I said, avoiding her eyes. "You have lovely things."

"I certainly hope to avoid the poorhouse," she said in a bright, chirpy voice that I knew was false. "I am lucky to have paid the year's lease in advance on the cottage, so I do not need to worry about shelter, at the very least."

My eye was drawn to a large leather scrapbook lying open on the desk next to the typewriting machine.

"I've kept copies of all my published pieces," said Mrs. Rattle, flipping over pages covered with pasted-in newspaper clippings. "My first job was at the *Toronto Telegram*, with 'Teatime Trifles, a Ladies Column.'"

"Wait," I said. "Let me –"

"The ladies of the Schubert Quartet enjoy great popularity, not only for their grand voices but because they study to please people . . ."

I read, and turned to the next one.

"In the garden of Mr. Jason Eggles, on Coburg Street, is a peach tree that has yielded over twelve baskets of fruit this year. Let me suggest how his wife might take best advantage of her bounty."

Then followed a recipe for peach cobbler.

"Aren't they ridiculous?" Mrs. Rattle laughed mournfully. "I had to write that foolish drivel for a full year before they let me hint that I possessed a brain. Then I began to find subjects who would add pepper to the picnic." She turned another page. "Here's one."

A SCIENTIST'S GRIM DISCOVERY

Dr. Casagrandi, in reading a paper before a medical association in Rome, stated that he had employed a number of women wearing long skirts to walk for one hour through the streets of the city. After the promenade, he submitted the skirts to a careful bacteriologic examination. There were found on every skirt large colonies of noxious germs, including those of typhoid fever, consumption, influenza, tetanus (or lockjaw), and numerous other bacilli.

Dr. Casagrandi maintained that women, and especially mothers, should at once discontinue wearing trailing skirts. Other members of the Medical Congress unhesitatingly passed resolutions to that effect.

That women should subject themselves to such filth has long been a wonder to those acquainted with bacteriology. Nevertheless, so long as fashion calls for long skirts, little reform can be expected, for the great majority of women are bound to be in the fashion regardless of any ordinary considerations. There is some encouragement, however, in the fact that many younger women of the present wear bicycle skirts or "bloomers" throughout the day and merely dress for dinner and the evening.

"Is that true?" I asked.

"Of course!"

"May I read more?" I asked.

"Well, yes, if you're really interested." Once again her expression darkened. "The *Telegram* claims that no one else was. That's why they ended my employ. 'Lack of reader interest.' They think women don't have time between cooking and sewing to read the newspaper, but they'll discover someday that we do. Isn't that right, Mable Riley? Perhaps the next time Mrs. Goodhand sends her loaf, you can use Underwood to transcribe some of your own stories."

"Oh!" I cried. "I have forgotten Mrs. Goodhand! Whatever is the time?" I had been at Silver Lining for hours and hours. I bid Mrs. Rattle a hasty farewell, thanking her over and over as I backed out the door, so that I must have appeared quite silly indeed.

The family was already at the table when I hurtled through the door. Eight eyes bore into me as I shed my shawl with my cheeks aflame.

"Dear Mrs. Goodhand, I apologize for being late." I bobbed a curtsy, not daring a glance at Viola.

"Punctuality is an acknowledgment of God," said Mr. Goodhand.

"Yes, sir" I said.

"If your attentions to the Widow Rattle have moved beyond charity, perhaps we need to consider how you might better be occupied," added Mrs. Goodhand.

"Yes, ma'am."

"Take your seat."

"Yes, ma'am."

And so ended my very favourite afternoon. I am tired past writing but will end simply with these words: When I am a grown woman, I vow to follow Mrs. Rattle's example and live every hour surrounded by loveliness and inspiration.

TUESDAY, SEPTEMBER 24

I am well pleased with myself this afternoon, for I have penned another rhyme for my scholars. In fact, I have decided to put my natural talent to use and author a special primer of my own.

Lesson 4 in the reader goes like this:

The jay cannot sing as well as the lark. The jay is a cross bird. It has a harsh voice. Bad boys and girls, like bad birds, do not like to sing. Good boys and girls like to sing. The hawk and the crow do not sing. Can you sing?

It made me chuckle to think what a "bad" bird might be. Here is my version:

> *The worms I bring, you will not eat*
> *The nest I've made, you won't keep neat*
> *You caw instead of singing sweet*
> *You are a bad, bad Jaybird!*

> *You tease the nestlings in the park*
> *You fly about when it is dark*
> *You cannot sing as well as Lark*
> *You are a bad, bad Jaybird!*

WEDNESDAY, SEPTEMBER 25

Because Wednesday is our "half day," school is dismissed at two o'clock instead of four. I asked Alfred if I might go to the post office with him in the afternoon. I hoped for another letter from Hattie.

Alfred is a pleasant young man, not at all frightening or peculiar as are most men of twenty. He asked about school and who was naughty or clever and whether Viola was very strict.

"The pupils in Miss Riley's classroom must consider themselves very lucky to have such a pretty and charming teacher," said Alfred.

"You need spectacles," I returned.

"When I was a boy, our teacher was Mr. Tamblyn, and never did you see such a pointed nose or a sharp tongue as that man had. Why, I do believe it were quicker to open letters with his nose than with a knife!"

We had quite a jolly ride and arrived in town before four o'clock.

I was impressed with my first real sight of Stratford. Because Viola and I had arrived in the evening, we did not see the town from the railroad station. Alfred claims that *nine thousand* people live in Stratford. He promised to bring me on a market day so that I may spend some hours looking about.

The courthouse, the city hall, and the post office seem all to have been built from the same load of bricks – red and yellow with much festive trim. The post office was very busy, with several townsfolk doing business or chatting when their business was done. I particularly remember there were a great many people because of what happened next. As Alfred and I made our way across the tiled floor, we heard someone call my name.

"Why, Mable Riley! What luck to see you here!" It

was Mrs. Rattle, wearing a cloak of scarlet cashmere, with violet gloves, which she waved at me wildly, as if summoning a child.

"I have good news to tell!" Her voice rang out like church bells on a cold night, and if that were not enough, she clasped me by the waist and kissed my cheek! It seemed to me that nine thousand pairs of eyes were staring at us. Alfred had edged away to speak with a clerk.

"What do you think? I have secured myself a job! My troubles will be lessened at once."

"A job?"

"Yes, beginning tomorrow at 6:40 A.M. I am to be a curd turner at the Bright Creek Cheese factory. How do you like that?"

"I – I –"

"What? Has the cat got your tongue?"

"No, ma'am. I – I am surprised, I think. I did not realize . . ." I looked at her elegant boots, her unpinned hair, and her luxurious cloak. "I am trying to picture you as a factory girl."

"I shall undergo a transformation, I assure you." She grinned. "I hope it won't be for terribly long, in any case.

"Oh, hello, Mr. Goodhand. Are you here to claim Mable?"

Alfred had inched his way back to my side.

"Mrs. Rattle has just become employed," I told him, "at the cheese factory."

"That's quite a distance to travel, ma'am," said Alfred, raising a rusty eyebrow. "Bright Creek is halfway to town from Sellerton."

"Oh, I'm well used to long journeys on my bicycle. It's only five or six miles. I can pedal that while I am still asleep!"

There were a few words more back and forth and then we came away, with Mrs. Rattle's "Come early on Sunday!" ringing in my ears.

Perhaps my behaviour was not admirable, but I believe I did not betray my mortification to Mrs. Rattle. I did not expect to see her there, in a public place.

Is it wrong to be ashamed in public about something that I secretly treasure? I would not give up my afternoons at Silver Lining for all the world, and yet – and yet how can I say this? I do not wish the world to know about them.

On the journey home, I sought to have Alfred's counsel on the matter.

"Alfred?"

"Hmmm?"

"What do you think of Mrs. Rattle?"

"Well, now, there's a question," said Alfred.

We trotted along in silence.

"Don't you think she's awfully pretty?"

"Hard to say what she looks like, her costumes are so distracting. A girl should look like a girl, in my opinion."

I giggled. "You sound like your father," I told him.

"There's times he's right," said Alfred. "No one wants to eat supper across the table from a gypsy. A man wants a girl in a tidy dress."

"My mother says we shouldn't judge people by their appearances."

"Well, I'm not saying she's wrong if you're referring to the appearance God gave us. I always thought my personality was more suited to something of a taller nature, with dark, wavy hair and a fine mustache."

Poor Alfred, I had never imagined a man might notice that he wasn't the handsomest.

"But it seems to me," he went on, "that in the matter of clothing and general upkeep, the way a person presents himself, or herself in this case, is an announcement to the world of who that person wants to be."

"I never thought of it like that," I said.

"With Mrs. Rattle, she's going to a heap of trouble to look peculiar, wouldn't you say? And making her point, I might add."

"I suppose."

That was all we said on the matter, but not all of what I thought about it. I expect the thinking will continue for as long as I know Mrs. Rattle.

THURSDAY, SEPTEMBER 26

When I awoke in the night, I was greatly comforted by Viola's back and the warmth of her beneath the quilt. I wished we might be friends again as we were when we were younger. That I might put my hand on the crook of her arm and not be pushed away. We used to play a game where I was the lost lamb and she was the blind shepherdess. It was silly, really. I would baa and hide and bleat, and she would find and comfort me.

I think what came between us was Papa's death. Mama needed Arthur to become the man of the house, though he was only fourteen. And she confided in Viola as she had not done before. Viola and Arthur became adults, and I was left to be a child. There was no more silly whispering at night, no more dressing up in Mama's petticoats, no more chatter or cuddling. I became a worry and a bother instead of a sister and a friend.

I wonder if Viola would agree with such speculation.

Finally, my efforts with the younger Cheerful Commas have paid off! We won the spelling bee to-day. We now trail by only twelve points! My own words, flawlessly spelled, were *miscellaneous, accommodate, allegiance,* and *condemned.* Elizabeth faltered on *condemned.* She used a double *m* instead of *m-n.* Ha!

Last evening we went again to Endeavor. (Elizabeth was quite civil, assuming perhaps that the Hyphens would triumph over the Commas this afternoon. Ha!)

Tommy Thomas was there, making us all laugh with his imitation of the Reverend Scott. He was very near discovered when Miss Robertson, at the piano, turned quickly to hide a sneeze and Tommy's fingers were wiggling at his chin like living whiskers. Elizabeth said he was showing off to impress me.

Alfred and Viola did *not* sing on the return walk. We were accompanied to the Elgin Road by a Mrs. Watson, whose husband owns the general store in Sellerton. She was only wed last spring and now expects the arrival of a baby before Christmas. She has a lovely soprano voice, but she tends to pant between verses.

When we parted ways, she invited Viola to go with her on Sunday next to a meeting of the new Ladies Reading Circle. Viola said she would think on it.

"It might be nice to make a friend or two for yourself," said Alfred as we walked on.

"Oh, I think not," said Viola. "I don't have time to read books, and what would the ladies think if the teacher was not even so clever as they are?"

"Reading a book may be just an excuse to get together for a gossip," said Alfred, quite kindly I thought. "In my mother's day, it was knitting for the needy."

"Perhaps," said Viola, but I could see she has no intention of going.

Joseph Brown chased me to-day during the lunch recess while his brother and Tommy watched from a perch in the oak tree. He pretended to think I had hidden his cap, but I saw it later in his satchel so have confirmed the ruse. I let him catch me next to the tree and dared him with my eyes to be impertinent. I should so like to know what it feels like to be kissed! But once he held my shoulders in his hands, he knew not what to do and slunk away with his ears bright pink.

The Brown boys are very sweet of face, but I suspect they may be lacking between the ears. Joseph is a Comma and Henry a Hyphen – they rather cancel each other out with their mistakes.

SATURDAY, SEPTEMBER 28

Wrote to Mama, wrote to Hattie, and then set about the labour of doing my laundry. The rain barrel is quite full from the recent storms, so I used rainwater, which is much nicer than from the pump. I washed both shirtwaists and all my stockings and underthings (which I did not hang in the yard! They dry on a rack in our bedroom). After less than an hour, the sun had done its work. I ironed the shirt-waists and hair ribbons and then wrote a postscript to Mama. I asked if we might afford the material for me to make a new shirtwaist.

I have calculated that Elizabeth has *six* shirtwaists, for she wears a different one every school day and a silk to church. I have two, and two collars. Even with the varying combinations, I must wear on Friday what has been already worn on another day! Perhaps I should improve my needlework with embroidering a new collar.

We heated more rainwater so that Viola and I could each wash our hair. She was in an amiable mood, so I helped curl her hair with the iron. It looks so pretty up in a knot, with a few curls purposely escaping. Alfred agreed with me, without prompting. If only she did not scowl so often.

The remainder of the morning I spent in writing another chapter for Hattie, to send with her letter, and another rhyme for my scholars, which I think is very clever.

When Frank awoke, he heard a <u>roar</u>.
It was so loud, it shook the <u>floor</u>.
He trembled as he listened <u>more</u>.
It surely was a dino<u>saur</u>!

Along the hall, Frank crept with <u>care</u>,
Alarmed by thunder in the <u>air</u>.
Imagining a growly <u>bear</u>,
Frank ventured to his parents' <u>lair</u>.

Poor boy was shaken to his <u>core</u>.
What monster lurked beyond the <u>door</u>?
Frank galloped in on the count of <u>four</u> . . .
There lay his father, caught mid-<u>snore</u>!

Will that not amuse them? And it makes good use of homophonic endings as well.

PART THE FOURTH
{THE DASHING CAPTAIN}

Helena knew not why her heart leaped as though lit with gunpowder, yet leap it did. A man stood in the doorway, the brim of his hat shadowing his face.

"Dear ladies and fine gentlemen." The man's smooth, deep voice set Helena's skin atingle. "This train will remain here only for the time it takes my associates to remove the sacks of gold and precious stones from the treasury car. It is my privilege to accept your watches and jewellery personally." He lifted his head as he stepped farther into the car.

Helena's breath caught in her throat. She had never seen anyone so handsome. He was clean-shaven, with dancing, dark eyes and a confident smile upon his full lips.

"Hey! Look here!" James pulled himself up, deciding too late to display some manliness. "Who do you think you are?"

The bandit turned his head and raised an eyebrow at the sight of James's flushed face and nervous hands.

"Yes, it's you I'm speaking to, you scurrilous rogue!" shouted James, raising his fists.

The stranger slid a firearm from the sash about his waist and pointed it lazily toward the ceiling.

"You may address me by name," spake he. "I am best known as Captain Brigand." Admiration thrilled through the car, for the title was well known in these parts. "Though I have heard," he continued with an impudent grin, "that officers of the law like to call me Ugly Joe."

With one swift motion he pulled the trigger on his gun, releasing such a burst of sound as to sting Helena's ears for several minutes.

"I have never yet killed a man," he said, "and surely do not want the first to be for reasons of stupidity. If you will all be so kind as to remove your valuables, I can do my job without causing harm."

The first glimmer of dawn's pink light cracked the shroud of darkness beyond the window. James slumped into his seat again, reaching into his pocket for his watch. Helena's fingers trembled at the clasp of her diamond brooch. It had been a birthday gift from her dear father, the earl, and was shaped like a crescent moon.

In an instant, the captain was before her, leaning close, the scent of him reminding her of saddles and wet grass on a spring morning. Helena raised her gentle green eyes to meet his dark ones for a prolonged moment of inner tumult. She placed her beloved trinket into his upturned palm and looked away.

It was only at that close range that Helena had

detected a dusting of boyhood freckles across the nose of the handsome bandit.

To be continued . . .

SUNDAY, SEPTEMBER 29

I went to Silver Lining straight from luncheon, following Mrs. Rattle's instruction to "come early." It was not until I started up her path that I realized I had left behind the customary loaf of corn bread! (It was not upon the table when I came home. I wonder that Mrs. Goodhand hasn't scolded me.)

The day was chilly but bright. I found her sitting on a wicker chair in the front garden, wrapped in the red cloak, with her face tipped toward the sun like a buttercup.

"Isn't sunshine the loveliest blessing on the planet?" she said, purring almost. "After three days without it, I must now replenish my spirit."

"Do you refer to your new job?" I asked. "Is it not what you hoped?"

She opened one eye in my direction, keeping her face tilted upward.

"It is unbearably tedious, suffocating, and unpleasant." She leaped up and extended her fingers for my inspection.

I could see how red and chapped they were, as if she had been scrubbing a whole castleful of floors.

"Ouch," I said.

"It's the salt," she said, "from turning the cheese curds for hours on end. The salt eats away under the nails. The other girls have given me a salve to soothe them, but it calms the skin for only a short while." She began to pace the garden path, looking anxious.

"I – I'm sorry, Mrs. Rattle. I forgot to bring the corn bread for the ducks."

"Ah, well," she said. "But you are here."

"Yes," I said, though she continued to move about without looking my way. Had she noticed my incivility at the post office and was paying me back?

"The factory work is harder than I expected," she admitted, sounding tired. "I knew it would be hard, but –" She flapped her hand as if giving up. "Ah, well. I mustn't complain. It will not be my whole life as it is for others. Such circumstances are set before us as one more trial to overcome."

I did not disguise my surprise at these words; she glanced at me and burst out laughing. "Why, Mable Riley! You think I am transformed into the Reverend Scott? I do not mean 'set before us' by God! No, indeed, far worse than that! Misery in the workplace is a *man*-made obstacle created for women of little means."

Oh dear, I thought. She might as well be Reverend Scott, for she fills her sermons with as many words as he does!

She did not invite me into the cottage to-day. I stayed only a short while longer in the garden and then walked home, most unsatisfied. As I came along the Elgin Road, I noticed Elizabeth lingering some way behind me. I stopped at the turn to see if she might catch up, but she darted off across the field instead.

I know not what to think of Elizabeth. If she weren't so bad tempered, her quick wit and cleverness would make her a good companion. Perhaps she is so self-absorbed there is simply no room for me.

TUESDAY, OCTOBER 1

This has been a black day, which I do not think is a good omen for the month of October. It began with burnt porridge, which was my doing, as Mrs. Goodhand asked me to stir while she went to the cellar for syrup. I hurried upstairs to retrieve my schoolbooks but did not return in time to prevent a scorched pot. It made a disgusting breakfast for all the household, but I pretended not to notice and ate mine up with exaggerated pleasure.

Viola puckered up her mouth as if it were full of poison and did not change her face all through the walk to school.

If Elizabeth had not ignored me in the cloakroom, I might have warned her of my sister's mood. But as she has shown no inclination for friendship, I left her unknowing. She spoke impertinently to Viola within minutes of the morning bell and was swiftly reprimanded.

"You will be detained after lessons to-day, Elizabeth," my sister announced, "doing every chore I can devise for your improvement."

"What makes you think that chores will improve me?"

Oooh, I thought, this girl has nerve!

Viola's chin seemed to sharpen with her anger. "You will also — Elizabeth? Stop jiggling. You are trying my patience to the utmost."

"Yes, Miss Riley."

"Repeat after me: 'I will not defy the teacher in manner or in word.'"

"I will not defy the teacher in manner or in word." Elizabeth's manner was decidedly defiant, which Viola chose to ignore.

"You have the words correct. You will write that sentence five hundred times and present me with the pages to-morrow morning. Now, class, the lesson continues. . . ."

My satisfaction in seeing Elizabeth punished lasted only until the reading hour, however.

The children were reading my new verse for the first

time. Ellen went first. "'When Frank awoke, he heard a roar. It was so loud, it shook the floor.'"

Then Irene. "'He trem . . . trem . . . bled,' oh! Trembled! 'As he listened more. It surely was a din . . . dine . . . dinosaur!'"

The children began to giggle. Now it was Frank's turn. "'A . . . along . . . the hall, Frank . . . cr . . . crep . . . crept . . . with . . . care. A . . . a . . . lar . . . ar . . . med . . .'"

"'Alarmed,' Frank! 'Alarmed!'" Ellen burst in.

"What are you reading, Frank?" Viola had appeared without warning.

"It's a poem, miss."

"What poem is it, Frank?"

"Mable made it, miss."

"The words in the book were dull, Miss Riley," volunteered Ellen, eager to fill in the story. "So Mable wrote new words for us. They're very funny, miss. About Frank's father." She had read ahead.

"We are not in school to be funny, Ellen. We are in school to read the words *in the book*, dull or not." She took the page from Ellen and scanned it silently, her cheeks reddening and her lips pinched together.

"Don't be angry," I pleaded. "It was only in fun, Viola, really."

She glared at me. "That's Miss Riley, if you please."

"I don't please," I said, though right away wished I hadn't, for her nostrils nearly split from quivering.

"Mable, you need to be reminded of your responsibility here." Her voice was as cold as ever I've heard it. "You will stay late with Elizabeth and perform extra duties in the classroom after lessons."

The children ducked their faces, pink with shame on my behalf. They were familiar with the dreadful feeling of awaiting a scolding. I could feel the eyes of the other scholars burning the back of my neck. I dared not look around to see what the boys might be thinking. I could only imagine the smirk on Elizabeth's face!

I wished to stick out my tongue at Viola, to shout and stomp my feet, but instead told the children to open their *Ontario Readers*. We finished the hour in a humbled drone.

"I'm sorry, miss," whispered Ellen as she departed for home. "It's a very good poem, anyway." I squeezed her hand and gave her a wink, so that she should not worry on my account.

Naturally, I expected a rebuke from Viola but was not prepared for the tongue-lashing I received. She hardly waited for the scholars to depart before she began. I cannot bear to repeat it all here. The worst was her opinion of my compositions.

"You call yourself an author? Ha! Childish rhymes that

ridicule the family members of your own scholars! Poetry should be graceful; it should glorify flowers or nature or God. And here you are, teaching rubbish about snoring! Homemade ridiculous rhymes! You have been placed in a position of trust, and you have displayed yourself to be entirely unworthy of that trust. The only thing that stopped me from strapping you to-day was the thought of our poor mama. What if Mrs. Forrest should hear of this? Insulting her husband in the name of education?"

On and on, more criticism for wasting time, for not obeying her instructions, for lacking talent . . .

My head aches just thinking of it, those hurtful words pouring over me while Elizabeth watched from her desk. Finally, Viola slowed her tirade and assigned us a formidable list of chores. Elizabeth and I began without speaking, both of us intent on finishing as quickly as we could.

At last there was left only the dull task of cutting strips of newspaper for use in the school privy. After asking Viola permission to work outdoors on the step, I imagined how peaceful it would be to send Elizabeth home.

"I can do the job alone," I said.

"And take credit where I gain none?" Elizabeth pouted at the thought.

"Come, then. There is one pair of scissors only. Would you like to fold or cut?"

We agreed upon our system and set to work with no further discourse, until she said, "I know where you were on Sunday."

I felt a quick heat flush my neck. Is that why I had seen her in the road upon my return from Silver Lining? Had she followed me? I wished to chide her but bit my lip instead. I had nothing to be ashamed of.

"It's not a secret," I murmured, making certain through the door that my sister was well occupied at her desk. "It's thanks to you that I've ever been there at all."

"You've not told my aunt the extent of it."

"I deliver the loaves, do I not?"

"Not always," said Elizabeth. "I hid the one you left behind on Sunday, for fear we'd have to eat it otherwise."

I stared at her and then laughed aloud. She grinned. I knew now why she'd followed me.

"Why should it matter if I keep company awhile?" I asked.

Elizabeth sighed but continued in a whisper.

"Have you been inside the cottage? Is it painted black within?"

I laughed again and covered my mouth at once lest Viola hear.

"Painted black? Of course not." The naked flying lady

was as pink skinned as Elizabeth. "Wherever did you hear such nonsense?"

"From my mother. Mrs. Forrest told her."

"What gain is there in telling lies about Mrs. Rattle?" I asked.

"I only wondered." Elizabeth reached for another newspaper and began to cut.

"It's true that Mrs. Rattle is an unusual woman," I said. "But there is no gain in slander." It hovered in my mind whether to state that I admired her beyond any other person. Instead, I made a plain reply. "She has the loveliest home I've ever seen. And nowhere did I see black."

Elizabeth studied me with an interest never before displayed.

"Did you locate her missing husband? Or hear about her family? Is it true she is estranged from them because of her unsuitable convictions?"

"That is not what she reports," I said, my voice sounding strange to my own ears. If only she had reported anything to me! If only I knew the secrets held within her bosom!

Viola coughed, startling us with a sound like a barking dog.

"Do you not wish," whispered Elizabeth, "that Mrs. Rattle could be your sister, replacing Miss Vile Riley?" She surprised me with a notion I had not yet had myself. As soon as it was spoken, I did wish it with all my heart.

It occurred to me that despite Elizabeth's disagreeable disposition, she displays more intelligence than any other scholar in Sellerton. We have also in common our loathing of Viola. Can such a thing be the foundation of a friendship?

Thinking to purchase an ounce of affection, I made a suggestion. "Elizabeth, I know a method for completing lines that will accomplish my sister's assignment in one-fourth the usual time."

She jumped to her feet with a bang, knocking our careful stack of privy papers into a storm of pamphlets. I jumped up myself, quite ready to scold her when I realized that Viola stood in the doorway. Elizabeth had created a distraction so that my plan should not be overheard! I crouched, giggling, to retrieve the papers and exchanged a look with her that sealed our conspiracy.

We bid a curt goodbye to Viola and set out together for the first time. Behind the Campbells' stable, we stopped at a thick stump flat enough to serve as a writing desk. I showed her the trick taught to me by Jimmy Fender, who certainly deserved the prize last year for the most lines written in punishment. He devised a method of holding two pencils in one hand, placing the leads on adjacent lines and writing two sentences concurrently.

"I shall do half the lines for you," I explained. "If we practise, our scripts will be like enough. I'm sure she will not examine them closely."

We agreed to meet before school in the morning, so that I could pass on my contribution. I did most of them before I began my entry tonight but must finish up now so as not to break my word. I pray Viola will not discover our game, for that would end Elizabeth's trust in me before it has truly taken root. (I suppose it is wrong to use prayer in making deceit be successful. I did not intend to involve God, just resolve.)

Though I have not decided yet to like Elizabeth, it is better by far to have her as a friend than to suffer the effects of her distemper.

WEDNESDAY, OCTOBER 2

It appears we have succeeded! Viola took the sheaf of papers from Elizabeth and handed them to me to count! I assured her it was a job well done, and she has not checked again that I can tell. Other than that, I have not spoken one word to Viola to-day but doubt that she has noticed. She is not speaking to me either.

It was Mrs. Goodhand's supper that prompted the rhyme I wrote tonight. Before the meal, I had been mulling over the text and vocabulary for Lesson 6:

> *How blessed are we with nature's feast,*
> *Brought forth by sun and gentle rain.*

. . . and so on. I had not a poetic thought in mind. But as I poked my vegetables and gnawed the beef, I was inspired. . . .

> *The sun doth shine on nature's feast*
> *And rain the earth doth feel,*
> *But by the fire*
> *'Tis cook's desire*
> *To ruin every meal.*

> *The beans are boiled till gray and limp,*
> *The meat is dry as dust.*
> *Potatoes lumpy,*
> *Custard bumpy,*
> *Yet blessings say, we must.*

LATER WEDNESDAY EVENING

I made the mistake of leaving my rough copies of the above verse on the bureau top while I visited the privy. Viola came upon them and went into a dreadful pucker! Have I not learned my lesson? What demon possesses me that I can write such wicked rhymes? (I confess, I shudder to think that Mrs. Goodhand might have chanced upon them, but I was spared that mortification.) Viola would not listen to reason, would not see the humour. She imagines we will be hurled into the Elgin Road with our trunks in the muddy ditch at our heels.

"If ever again I find that you have defied me in this, Mable, I will have you scrubbing the schoolhouse floor until your fingers are too raw to hold a pencil!"

I must take better care that she does not find my notes again!

Part the Fifth
{Helena's Escape Discovered}

Meanwhile, Helena's homely sister had awakened in her enormous boudoir, to the sound of the bronze clapper falling repeatedly against the mahogany front door.

"Whoever can that be?" Myrtle's voice was like that of a fearful piglet, high and wobbling. She wondered where her slovenly maid was hiding. (Myrtle's maid, Elizabeth, never expecting her mistress to awaken before ten o'clock, was behind the stable, flirting with the undergroom.)

Hurriedly, Myrtle pulled on her robe (of a most unsuitable color) and scuttled down the stairs like a kitchen rat.

"Why ever are you pounding on the door, you dreadful man?" Myrtle squinted viciously at the person hovering anxiously on the step. "Have you no respect for the noble family that sleeps within?"

"It is that very respect that brings me here, miss," said Mr. Edwards, the stationmaster. "Your sister is departed on the midnight train, led astray by a scoundrel."

"Are you intoxicated, fool?" chided Myrtle.

"I've not taken a drink since me brother died of it, eight years ago," said Mr. Edwards, his feelings hurt. "I saw what I saw. The Lady Helena boarded the 12:01 and she weren't alone. I'd rather have told your father, the earl, only I don't want to be breaking his heart." With these sad words, Mr. Edwards turned away and trudged back over the snowy road, following his own tracks home.

Myrtle closed the door more thoughtfully than she had opened it. Could it be true? Could her despised, angelic sister have taken so wrong a step? What good fortune was this! Helena the Perfect would now be cast out of the family, leaving the riches, the manor, and their father's love to Myrtle, and only Myrtle. Oh, happy day! How best to celebrate?

"Elizabeth!" Myrtle called so loudly that the whining shriek reached even to the stable. The immoral maid hastened to pluck the straw from her hair as the undergroom leered at her rosy lips.

"Come back when you've put your lady in the bath," he said greedily. "I cannot wait until tonight for another taste of your kisses."

Elizabeth giggled and hurried away to do her mistress's bidding.

"Where have you been, you lazy hussy?" demanded Myrtle, but not waiting for an answer, gave rapid orders. "Draw my bath, prepare the rose oil and dusting powder, display my favourite dresses for selection, and bring my breakfast immediately. I want four eggs, twelve griddlecakes with maple syrup, three currant scones with marmalade, a bowl of strawberries, and a pot of the finest China tea. You may also notify my father, the earl, that I request a special audience this morning."

"But, Lady –"

"What?" Myrtle glared.

"It's the dead of winter. There is no strawberries nowhere."

Myrtle's voice dropped to a chilling hiss. "I said strawberries."

To be continued . . .

Ambler's Corner
September 30, 1901

My dear girls,

When I am missing you most, I comfort myself that you have each other for company. Only that thought can gladden my heart.

I am stealing a few moments to write while Teddy and Flossie do their schoolwork at the kitchen table next to me, sharing the lamp. Bea is in bed, and never was a mother happier to have a scrappy chick washed and sleeping. Without you two here to help, my evenings are endless: washing up, sweeping the kitchen (after Flossie has swept and spread the crumbs instead of gathering), kneading tomorrow's bread, scouring the hearth, filling the buckets, not to mention the parade of tired children resisting night-dresses, tooth powder, hairbrushes, face flannels, misplaced dollies, boots to wipe, pinafores to sponge, stories, and, finally, prayers.

It is not the younger children who are keeping me up at night, however. . . . I refer to your brother Arthur and his fancy for a certain young lady. He is a fine boy, if I do say so myself, but to be blunt, we do not have the social standing that the Melbournes might expect for their Laura. I am worried that he will be cast aside after a few pleasant hours on their porch swing.

The most a mother can hope for any of her children is that they are lucky enough to find a companion who will share a contented home.

Until then, you have each other.

Much love,

Your mother

Finally a spelling bee to crow about, despite a bad beginning. We were lined up along the wall as usual. The little ones went first and each did well. So when Cathy made her error, I regretted not being close enough to pinch her.

"Ooooh!" she wailed. "I meant to say it *s-t-u-b-b-o-r-n*, Miss Riley! Honestly, I did! My tongue just got confused and omitted the second *b*."

"Next time you'll take a moment to compose your tongue before speaking," said Viola.

Cathy stopped her noise with a gulp. "My mother will not be pleased," she whispered.

"Next word, Henry Brown. *Dauntless*. Can you spell *dauntless?*"

Of course, Henry spelled it *d-o-n* and he was out. By a miracle, Joseph (on my team) made no error, nor did anyone but Cathy. The Cheerful Commas were cheerful indeed as we won the day!

I have been giving mother's letter some thought. Her fancy that Viola and I are good companions to each other is so far from the truth that I know not whether to laugh or to hang my head in shame. It *would* be best if we were friends. What better than to have a confidante who has been witness to one's entire life? The trouble being, with Viola and me, that we are not confidantes. At present, I cannot spill the secrets of my heart for fear of a harsh laugh or an admonishment. Quite possibly she, too, has secrets that she does not share with me (though I cannot imagine what!).

I wish that Viola were a more laudable person, like Mrs. Rattle, that I might emulate her example and be praised instead of chastized for my efforts. I feel bursting in my skin and cannot wait until Sunday to go once more to Silver Lining.

SATURDAY, OCTOBER 5

I found myself following Alfred about the barn this evening like a puppy after the butcher's boy. I tried to moan about Viola, but Alfred would hear no complaints.

"You're a lucky girl to have such a fine sister," he said, scooping pitchforkfuls of hay into the cattle stalls. "My own sister, Thora? Her husband inherited a farm in Manitoba so they live four hundred miles away. She has two children I've never met."

"That would suit me just fine," I grumbled.

He paused to wipe the sweat from his red face with the back of his hand. "Family is the best thing we have on this earth. Your mother shows courage in letting her daughters go off into the world to make a life for themselves. You'd best make the best of it. She doubtless feels more than four hands short without the two of you."

"That's true," I said. But Alfred was distracted.

"Will you scoot into the kitchen and bring me the pan of water boiling on the stove?" he asked. "Tildie here has managed to get a wedge lodged in her leg. I need to pull it out." He slapped the side of one of the cows.

When I returned, carefully balancing the hot iron pot with both hands in oven mittens, Alfred had led the cow out of her stall and set up a stool next to her.

"She must have scraped up against something," he said. "There's a bit of a gash. See here? You see that tip? That's a piece of fence post or tree branch, maybe." He soaped his hands and rinsed them and washed the cow's wound with warm suds.

"Lucky it's a foreleg," he murmured. "Less chance of getting myself kicked. You can help, if you would, Mable. Keep stroking her. Whisper a bit, keep her calm."

After a minute or two of nonsense, I could not think what to say to a cow so I repeated the Lord's Prayer in the most soothing tone I could muster. I was riveted by Alfred's fingers, which look so thick and freckly normally and now were transformed into deft tools. He gently spread the opening with one hand and grasped the object, using a small pair of pliers. Tildie bellowed and stamped.

"Thy will be done on earth," I whispered, "as it is in Heaven."

"Ha!" cried Alfred. "Got it!" He pulled out the pliers, gripping an oversize splinter of bloodied wood. "Pass me that jug of witch hazel, would you?"

He poured it over the wound and wrapped a strip of cotton around the leg. "Good girl," he said, giving Tildie a rub between the ears. "Milking time!" He led her back to the stall and sat down again with the pail between his feet and his forehead pressed into the cow's side. She mooed, and shortly the lowing echoed up and down the barn.

"Do you milk all twenty cows by yourself?" I asked.

Alfred chuckled. "I'd never get in to supper if I did that. My father will be along in a minute, and we'll have our usual race." He began to gently knead the cow's teats.

The barn door creaked and the light shifted as Mr. Goodhand came in carrying two silver milk pails.

"Huh," he grunted. Perhaps he thought he said hello. I jumped to my feet as he scowled. "Milking time is not social time, Mable. I'm sure Mrs. Goodhand could use your help in the kitchen."

"Yes, sir."

And I was off, with a quick wink from Alfred to see me across the yard. I tried to imagine what he might be like in thirty years. Will he lose his good cheer and become a gruff old man like his father?

Later, as we were clearing the table after supper, Elizabeth and Mrs. Campbell hurried in.

"Have you had a letter from Mother?" Mrs. Campbell asked Mrs. Goodhand, not even sitting down before she spoke.

"Alfred didn't get over to the post office to-day."

"Father's taken very poorly," announced Mrs. Campbell, and then she began to cry, in great, gulping sobs.

Elizabeth leaped forward and eased her mother into a chair. I felt tears well up in my own eyes and glanced at Viola. Though different words were used, the report of a sick father shot me back to the evening in our own Ambler's Corners kitchen when Arthur had come home with similar news. I saw from her whitened lips that Viola bore the same memory, but she did not meet my eye.

Mrs. Goodhand reached out to take the letter from her sister's shaking hand. Her husband stood behind her, reading over her shoulder, mouthing the words as he squinted to read in the poor light.

"One of us will go to help Mother with the nursing," resolved Mrs. Goodhand, folding the letter.

"One of us? Why, both must go at once." Mrs. Campbell hiccuped.

"Hazel will go tomorrow." Mr. Goodhand decided the

matter in his customary fashion. "If he is not recovered in ten days' time, you will go and my wife will return."

"But –"

"You cannot leave Elizabeth alone, with your husband gone from dawn till dusk. Alfred and Viola are both here to look after the farm with me."

I saw Viola's eyebrows lift, but she did not argue.

Mrs. Goodhand bore her sister's anguish without flinching. "I believe Howard is right," she said. "Stop your fussing now, Marion. You'll only distress yourself."

I had a sudden picture of Mrs. Goodhand and Mrs. Campbell as young women, the former looking like Alfred wearing an apron and being a Bossy Boots to her little sister, just as Viola is to me.

In the bedroom, later, Viola paced back and forth, adjusting the curtain, smoothing the quilt, blowing dust from the bureau top.

"He might have asked me," she complained. "We are paying boarders, after all. It is not up to me to keep the farm running. There will be all the watering to do, the cleaning, the baking, and the cooking. . . . You will have to help me, Mable. At home even more than at school."

"I'd rather eat your cooking than Mrs. Goodhand's," I said.

She grinned at me. "Oh, Mable, that's true! She's quite the worst cook who ever sliced a cabbage. We shall feast while she's away!"

SUNDAY, OCTOBER 6

The sermon was "God Prefers Us to Be Cheerful," but I am certain that God looked upon the Goodhand and Campbell families this morning and made an exception.

Mrs. Goodhand made a cold plate lunch and then filled a basket to the brim with provisions for her parents and set off with her husband in the wagon to drive to Berlin. As soon as we had waved them off, I tidied the dishes and made ready to depart for Silver Lining.

"Where do you suppose you're going?" asked Viola.

"To visit Mrs. Rattle."

"Mrs. Goodhand did not bake this morning. There is nothing to take for her."

And so I stood, my shawl around my shoulders and my brain not summoning a reason that I still might go.

"I-I-It is my visiting more than the loaves that brings her pleasure."

"That idea disturbs me greatly. It is widely known that this woman is a crackpot. Perhaps she is the cause of your insolent rhymes? I cannot risk the effect she is having on your behaviour, Mable. I forbid you to go there again."

"You cannot forbid me! You are not my mother!"

"Thank Heaven for small mercies. Now, if you'll excuse me, there's work to be done." And she stomped into the yard, swinging a bucket as if to snap the handle.

"Your sister can certainly use some help," said Alfred gently. "We're short all 'round to-day." He tweaked my hair as he went out, not knowing he had pulled a gray curtain across my sunny day.

I did my chores in silence, and have come upstairs to fume. How dare Viola tell me where I may or may not visit! I have missed Silver Lining to-day, but I shall not miss it again. Perhaps I need not tell my sister when I plan to pay a call?

MONDAY, OCTOBER 7

I meant not to speak to Viola until Christmas, but we have come to a truce out of necessity. She suggested that I choose friends of my own age and keep my "high spirits" under control. I made several declarations of good intentions, thinking that the shortest path to peace.

After this exchange of dubious sincerity, Viola and I pretended to be farm wives making the supper for Alfred and his father. It was served late, for we could not put the chicken in to roast until we were home from school, but Mr. Goodhand quit his grumblings as soon as the first forkful met his mouth. Indeed, I have never seen him smile at the table before now. Alfred was beside himself – "The dumplings are so light! The gravy so rich! Such an apple tart!" – until he realized his compliments were also insults to his absent mother. Viola was quite pink with triumph and whispered to me later that we have been trained well to win favour with our cooking.

"Will you listen to this," said Mr. Goodhand from his stove-side chair after supper. "Hazel's in the paper and not here to enjoy it.

> **"Mrs. Howard Goodhand has left the village to visit for several days with her parents in Berlin. Her father, Mr. Horace Finchley, is ailing.**

"And let's hope this next one is not an omen.

> **"Mr. Wm. Nichols has returned from Toronto, where he was taking the annual training in embalming."**

"That's gruesome," said Viola.

"I suppose it's a good thing there's a school for it," said Mr. Goodhand. "I want someone who knows his business when it's my time come along."

"That's not a family business I'd be wanting to take over," said Alfred. "I'm glad we've got a farm."

"Hey, listen up," said Mr. Goodhand. "Here's someone you know, Mable.

"A meeting of the Ladies Reading Circle will take place on Sunday afternoon at the home of Mrs. Cora Rattle. All ladies are welcome. Refreshments will be served."

"Do these women have nothing better to do all day than read stories?" asked Alfred.

"Seems to be spinsters and widows mostly," said Mr. Goodhand. "No one with a husband to care for is sitting about the kitchen with a book in her hand. There's no man I know that wants to come home to a dose of poetry. You keep that in mind, Mable."

"Mable is still at an age where a friend seems more important than a husband," said Viola.

"I cannot truly claim her for a friend," I protested meekly. I fled upstairs as soon as the washing up was done.

I am not easy, knowing my intention is to deceive my sister and pursue Mrs. Rattle for my friend. But when I think upon the alternative, of seeing her no more – I realize there is no choice.

I have written another episode of my romantic novel for Hattie. I find I want to fill it with exotic details that will shock her and make her scold me.

Part the Sixth
{The Captain's Companion}

Helena gazed into the eyes of her captor, but she was given no time to submit to bewilderment. Captain Joseph Brigand bowed low as he departed the carriage. The gentlefolk aboard the train were herded into the last car and kept under the guard of a lowly villain named Whiphand Pete.

Huddled in a corner were two young children, cared for by an elderly woman. The boy and his sister cried pitifully, while the old woman, with bonnet askew, held them close and sang quietly.

"Shut yer mewling," growled Whiphand Pete, "or I'll plug yer throats with me boot!" He waved his firearm in the air.

James twitched at Helena's side, and she feared he would take matters into his own feeble hands. Her heart fluttered like a sparrow frightened by a barn cat, but she found courage in the need to protect the children.

"Hear me, sir! I will speak with your captain," she demanded.

"Heh, heh, heh," chortled Whiphand Pete. "A feisty one, eh?"

"There is no call to be rude, sir, nor will I permit you to terrify the children needlessly. I must have words with your leader." And with that, our brave Helena gathered her skirts and swept past Whiphand Pete toward the door.

"Wait a minute there, little hussy!" the bandit cried. He threatened her with his pistol but could not pursue her for he risked being overcome by the other prisoners. Helena's sweet red lips strove to hide her smile of triumph.

The door was heavy for Helena's womanly strength, but fueled with determination, she flung it open. The wind of a wintry dawn slapped her face like an angry governess, and she caught her breath in surprise. Her attention went to the two men in black coats speaking confidentially together with their backs to her.

Helena stepped from the train ladder and made her way toward them. She recognized the leather hat of Captain Brigand, and she addressed herself to his broad shoulders.

"Captain?" Her voice, which she had intended to be resolute, rang forth like the tone of a cracked bell.

When he turned, Helena was astonished once again by the comeliness of the man before her. His eyes were such a deep, magnetic brown that she felt her body sway toward him.

"Are you ill, madam?" His voice held the concern wished for by every young bride.

"No, no!" Helena lifted her chin to enforce some self-command. "I am here to complain about the actions of your compatriot. He treats us in a most repugnant manner, threatening old ladies and scaring the children."

"He is a train bandit, my dear," said Captain Brigand with a teasing smile. "However, he seems to have permitted your escape. Should you not be trembling?"

"It is enough that you have robbed me, sir. I will not be insulted as well." With every beat of her heart, she fought the desire to throw herself into the man's arms.

So spellbound was Helena that she had disregarded the captain's companion, until he spoke.

"Joseph?"

Helena's head spun as she looked at the speaker. Except for a needle-sharp line scarring his cheek, this man was an exact twin of Captain Brigand. The same flashing walnut-brown eyes, the same full lips, the same fine face.

"Meet my brother," said the captain with a warm laugh. "We call him Pretty Harry."

To be continued . . .

TUESDAY, OCTOBER 8

The evening meal was once more a success. We used the remains of yesterday's chicken to make a splendid pie. Alfred's friend Roy helped out with hauling to-day, so we had an extra for supper. And then Mrs. Campbell arrived with Elizabeth as we finished the rice pudding.

"You've not had a note to-day, I suppose?" she asked. "My sister should know we're waiting for word."

"She'll be busy at the sickbed," said Mr. Goodhand, though he'd been complaining of the same thing himself during the meal. "We'll hear tomorrow."

"If you were the butcher, Aunt Hazel could call you on the telephone," said Elizabeth. "He advertises in the newspaper that he has a telephone, have you noticed? 'For Good

Meat, phone 91.' She could call us to say if Grandfather is any better."

"Well, I'm not the butcher, am I?" gruffed Mr. Goodhand. "No point in foolish fancy."

"The telephone is getting popular for a reason, Dad," said Alfred.

"I've seen them work," said Roy. "My uncle has one."

"It *would* make things simpler now," sighed Mrs. Campbell. "But what will the world have come to when a farm cottage in Perth County has a telephone cable poking out of it!"

"Would it not be a lark, though?" I said. "We could telephone to our mother to say hello whenever we think of her! Or, instead of traipsing across the field tonight, Elizabeth could just have telephoned to ask for news!"

"That's all we need!" groused Mr. Goodhand. "For every woman in Canada to be armed with a telephone! There'd be no work done and no dinners cooked. The hours of wasted chatter would bring about the downfall of the country! Not to mention if giggling girls were to get their hands on such an instrument. Lord be!" And with that, he pushed his chair away from the table and supper was ended.

THURSDAY, OCTOBER 10

We heard yesterday from Mrs. Goodhand that her father is very weak. He has such trouble breathing that she and the doctor have constructed a tent to fill with steam to ease the congestion in the patient's chest. Elizabeth says her mother is distraught at being left home, so far away from her ailing father.

I received a letter of my own to-day!

Silver Lining

Dear Miss Mable Riley,

I am hosting this Sunday's meeting of the Ladies Reading Circle and would be most appreciative of your assistance in serving the tea.

Please inform if this should cause inconvenience for you or your guardians. The meeting begins at three o'clock, but I hope to see you as soon after lunch as you are able to come.

Affectionately,
Cora Rattle

My first typewritten letter! And see what a flourish she has made of her signature! Using violet ink! I was trembling as I folded the letter and tucked it into this journal. Already the questions raced into my head, fighting for attention: Will Viola let me go? How to convince her? Happily Mrs. Goodhand is away, else she might deal the deciding blow.

LATER

This keen battle with Viola has taught me what our statesmen must apply to any disagreement. I went to her and showed the invitation, without a prologue. She merely shook her head and reminded me of her decision to stop my liaison with Mrs. Rattle.

Here is where I shone. I did not lose my temper or speak in haste, but cajoled instead. Was this not an opportunity for me to witness ladies in society? Could I not benefit from their manners in designing my own? Would it not be elevating to hear a discussion of literature? If I were to prove my maturity, by assisting my sister with good humour from this moment on, oh, please, Viola! Pretty, pretty please?

And I won! She consented! I am to go!

Oh, what shall I wear? If only I had a new shirtwaist! What if I drop a teacup or tip the cakes into someone's lap? Should I try to join the conversation or remain silent, like a servant? How will I make certain to be asked there again? How to put forth the best Mable Riley?

FRIDAY, OCTOBER 11

Alfred took a note for me to Mrs. Rattle to-day, accepting her invitation. It did not say what I feel, which is this:

HOW WILL I EVER WAIT
UNTIL SUNDAY???

(Hesitating Hyphens total to date: 79
Creeping Closer Commas: 76)

PART THE SEVENTH
{THE EARL RECEIVES THE NEWS}

While Myrtle gobbled her sumptuous breakfast, she began to plot the revenge she'd always dreamed of having on her lovely sister.

"Have the valet tell my father that I wish to speak with him," Myrtle ordered her maid, Elizabeth. "I have news that will spin his poor doddering head back to front."

With that scornful prophesy came cackling laughter that could scarcely be described as human, let alone ladylike.

Another hour passed before Myrtle was content with her hair, her dress, her jewels, her scent, and finally pronounced herself ready to address her father, the earl. She did not notice the valet roll his eyes before he announced, "The Lady Turtle, I mean, Myrtle, my lord." (The earl was shortsighted as well as quite deaf, so he did not notice, either.)

"Good morning, Myrtle dear," said the earl.

"You look dreadful, Father," said Myrtle, looking upon him with little interest. "Are you poorly?"

"Eh?"

"Are you SICK, Father?" shouted Myrtle.

"I did not sleep. I was kept awake by my concern for your dear sister. I can't think what has kept her from my side since yesterday."

"Indeed, the reason is not one you would think of," replied Myrtle with a sneer.

"Eh?" cried the earl. "How you mumble, child!"

"I know where Helena is!" hollered Myrtle.

"No need to bellow like a barmaid, my dear," said the earl. "Where is she, then?"

"She has run away!" cried Myrtle, hardly containing her glee. "She has eloped with a scoundrel and departed on the midnight train! What do you say about your precious Helena now?"

But Myrtle was unprepared for the consternation that flustered the earl. He staggered back, his face ashen. One hand groped for a chair, and the other clutched his chest.

"Hawkins!" Myrtle screamed for the valet.

The loyal servant burst into the room and hurried to his master's aid. The earl's eyes rolled back in their sockets as Hawkins laid him down upon the chesterfield.

"You must summon Dr. Mettle at once, my lady. I know not what you said to his lordship, but it appears you've about killed him."

To be continued . . .

SATURDAY, OCTOBER 12

I have fulfilled my duties as Viola's slave this morning – we made all the bread for the week (fourteen loaves). Then she kindly assisted me in doing pear tarts for Mrs. Rattle's meeting tomorrow, before we baked a cake for Mr. Goodhand's tea.

We did not mention my outing again, but I wonder if she is a bit envious. Not that I am going, but that she is not. I think sometimes that Viola's sharpness is a cover for shyness – she would falter if asked to offer an opinion about a book. Opinions are much more difficult to put forth than facts.

SUNDAY!!! OCTOBER 13

I knew when I awoke this day that I would see and hear much of interest at Mrs. Rattle's gathering but did not expect to return home with my brain on fire.

I arrived at Silver Lining before two o'clock, perspiring though the wind was cold. I worried that Mrs. Rattle's face looked drawn and there were gray smudges under her eyes, but she hugged me in gratitude for coming and I saw at once that she needed my help. My tarts were most welcome, as her own attempt at baking had resulted in scorched biscuits and a fallen cake.

"I have never baked a cake in all my life," she explained. "As a child, I watched Cook do it every afternoon, but clearly I have forgotten an important detail." She giggled and pointed at her sunken failure. Her hands were still as rough and red as they'd been the other day.

"We could make a trifle," I said, "if you have any fruit. And some cream. We'll line the pudding with the best bits from your cake." Her gaze of admiration warmed my cheeks.

"That's why I like you, Mable Riley. You know how to do things."

"Anyone can make a trifle," I said.

"Not true," she answered. "I have never made a trifle. Or a cake. But I shall learn, I swear it. There is a saying, 'The richest women are the most useless.' I am determined to break this rule and become useful. That is my goal – in the kitchen as well as in the world."

I was momentarily dumbstruck.

"But you're not rich," I said. "You work in a factory."

"I am from a wealthy family," she said, "and therefore completely untrained in the skills required for independence." She handed me six wizened peaches, which I set about to scalding. I made the trifle as best I could, and suddenly it was three o'clock and the ladies were arriving.

There were seven of them in all.

I was expecting Mrs. Watson from the choir, of course, but was astonished to see Miss Robertson, who does the church accounts for Reverend Scott. She has spectacles so thick she might use them for doorknobs. There were two women from Sellerton I had not met: Miss Thomas (with manly eyebrows) and her sister, Mrs. Tupper, whose husband has a large piggery on the other side of the village.

The most surprising was the last to arrive. It was Helen! I think of her as Kissing Helen (from the train station on our first evening). She arrived with a friend called Mrs. Sophie Barnes, and I could see at once that they were not so genteel as the other ladies. (Or am I adding that now that I have heard her story?) Helen Stevens did not seem so lovely standing in Mrs. Rattle's parlor as she did in the arms of her beloved. It was a shock to examine her closely. Her complexion was dull, the ribbon on her hat was stained, and her cuffs were frayed. How could this be my heroine, brimful of love and adventure?

Sophie wiped her palms on her skirt as they hovered in the doorway. When they caught sight of the naked dancer on the wall, they eyed each other, hiding giggles behind their hands.

"Come in, come in, Helen, my dear," said Mrs. Rattle. "Sit here, Sophie, next to Miss Robertson. Mable will bring you a cup of tea."

I did so at once, while Mrs. Rattle continued. "This is Helen Stevens and Sophie Barnes, everyone. They have come all the way from town to-day on their day off, just to confirm that what I tell you is true. They work at the Bright Creek Cheese Company and have been there much longer than I have."

The ladies oohed and aahed as if this were very important news, and the factory girls wriggled under their scrutiny. Where was Helen's Phillip to-day? Had he driven them over? I looked out the window but saw no mustached man loitering in the garden.

Other than Mrs. Rattle, all the women appeared ordinary. (Only later did I consider this with more attention.) They wore neat, dark clothing; their hats were fashionable but not showy. Their hair was pinned, their manners pleasant, and their chatter gay and friendly.

I poured the tea, asking each time, "One cube or two?" and slid a dainty silver spoon into the saucer.

"This is Mable Riley," announced Mrs. Rattle, patting my shoulder. "She is a neighbour and a very clever young woman. She brought the pear tarts *and* made the trifle! I thought she might benefit from our discussion here to-day. Her *sister*" – she emphasized the word "sister," which surprised me. She has never met Viola that I know of – "is the new schoolmistress."

"How very helpful that would be," murmured Miss Thomas.

"A delicious trifle, my dear Miss Riley!" said Mrs. Tupper. "Our brother's son, Tommy, is in your class and often speaks of you. Quite a favourite with the boys, I hear."

I wished I were not gripping the teapot so that I could cover my face.

"Oh, don't blush, child! It will serve you well to win the hearts of men. So long as you win their votes as well, isn't that right, girls?" She looked around and the other ladies laughed. "Isn't that what we're here for?"

Indeed, I realized at that moment that none of them carried a book or had mentioned reading once. I put the teapot back under its cozy. Was this not the Ladies Reading Circle?

No! It was not!

When Mrs. Rattle called the ladies to order, I discovered myself in the midst of a meeting of suffragists! This was a secret club! The Reading Circle is but a ruse to hide their real intentions from husbands and busybodies.

Had I been suspended upside down from the peak of a hay wagon, I could not have felt more sick. Yet thrilled as well, I confess it. Hattie would never believe me! Viola could not imagine it! But what did they mean about Viola being helpful? She had been afraid to join even the Reading Circle when Mrs. Watson had asked! How could she help anything? What would she think to find herself where I was! And where was I? Why had I been invited?

I refilled the teacups, not breathing for fear I'd miss something.

Mrs. Rattle readied her pencil above a small notebook. "We'll begin with a short report on your activities since the last meeting," she said, "and then attend to the business of Bright Creek. Agatha, you first."

Miss Thomas sat up tall, like a scholar preparing to recite. "I have ordered the fabric for our pennants. Your husband, Mrs. Watson, was most curious as to what I might be doing with twenty yards of felt. I do think it best that we did not involve you. He said I should receive the shipment within the week."

"Very good," said Mrs. Rattle. "We can use our meeting times to cut and stitch. If we're not making enough progress, we'll work at home in between. Though daylight hours at home are now a luxury. Thyra?" She turned to Miss Robertson, who nervously adjusted her spectacles.

"It has been a most trying week," said Miss Robertson. "I did not approach the Stratford Council as I had intended. Mr. Scott has been ill and requiring attention like a baby . . ." Her voice trailed off in admission of failure.

"Any likely recruits this month, Muriel?" Mrs. Rattle addressed Mrs. Watson, who hesitated and looked at me before speaking.

"I am becoming friendly with the new teacher, Miss Riley, as she goes to Endeavor with me on Thursdays." She then turned to me. "I did not realize you would be here, Mable. I am hopeful that your sister will join our ranks. What do you think? Is your sister of a like mind with us?"

My throat went dry. What could I say? That Viola would rather run ten miles in wet skirts than be a suffragist?

"Do you understand, Mable?" said Mrs. Rattle, as if she were speaking to a Grade One scholar. "The teacher is a respected member of any small community. We need supporters who might have influence with many families. Do you suppose your sister . . . ?"

Is *that* why I was invited? To woo Viola to participate in this peculiar assembly? Is *that* why Mrs. Rattle has been friendly to me?

I took a sip of tea, which had gone cold in my cup. "I think my sister is, uh, still perhaps, uh, getting used to her new position." I sounded like a dimwit but could not prevent myself. "Perhaps you should, uh, wait awhile longer to approach her." I was addressing Mrs. Watson, but the sigh of disappointment was from everyone. I never wished harder to be hidden under my quilt than at that moment.

"Well, then, Muriel," said Mrs. Rattle, "continue to be friendly, and we'll discuss it again at the next meeting. Now I would like to say a few words." She stood up to speak.

"When I moved to Stratford, I planned to live on my savings until I could find employment with the newspaper. That employment has not come. I have become a curd presser instead and realize I have been pampered and blind until this month of my life. I did not expect to be a labourer and I do not enjoy being a labourer, but I am grateful for the opportunity to have my eyes opened wide. I will never again eat a piece of cheese or wear shoes or use soap without wondering what hardships were faced by the women who made those things!"

She raised her voice as if addressing the audience in a town hall rather than a circle of ladies in her own parlour. "Women are the victims of a universal scandal! But here at the Bright Creek Cheese Company, we have a chance to open more eyes, to improve the working conditions for our own neighbours! Tell them, girls." She beckoned to Helen Stevens and Sophie Barnes. "Is it not time for change?"

The factory girls seems a little cowed at first by the force of Mrs. Rattle's passion, but she soon had them talking about what their work involved.

"I've been there two months," said Helen.

"I've been there more than a year," said Sophie.

"We start at 6:40." said Helen. "I'm up at five in time to walk out to the factory. With the walk, I'm home by eight o'clock in the evening."

"My mother looks after my kiddies," said Sophie. "I'm lucky that way."

"I'm usually on the stir vat," said Helen, "meaning I handle the pole and move the curds around without stopping or they clot."

"All day," said Mrs. Rattle. "Just as I spend my twelve hours in the next room, working the curd press. And Sophie's on cleaning. Show them your arms, Sophie."

Obediently, Sophie unbuttoned her cuffs and rolled back her sleeves, revealing wicked lashes, inflamed and blistered.

"The burns don't have a chance to heal," she explained. "The water's got to be boiling, to sterilize the milk cans, but they don't give us gloves or naught and the soap is harsh."

"But what can we do?" Mrs. Watson sounded bewildered. "Why do you not explain to the boss what the problems are?"

"We need our jobs," said Helen. "Mr. Forrest knows that. I was meant to be getting married, but Phillip's gone off and left me. I need every penny."

I tried not to stare. It was hard enough to accept that Helen was not as romantic as I had imagined. But to find her alone and miserable made me feel actually sick. Is this how Mrs. Rattle would be in a few weeks' time? Hopeless and exhausted?

I busily collected the cups and plates to wash up. The tray jiggled so much in my trembling hands that the sugar bowl and creamer did a dance. In the kitchen, I purposely clattered and clanked so as not to hear any more. I could not absorb another word. A thousand thoughts stormed my mind. I felt tossed, as if by waves, and prayed for the wind to drop to allow some peace of mind.

I could not wait for the meeting to conclude. The refreshments were done with, the dishes tidied. Grateful that I'd left my shawl draped across the kitchen chair, I took it and slipped out the back door.

A drizzle had begun, and the smell of wet leaves was stirred up by my feet as I hurried home through the dusk. I thought how to explain my afternoon. "They were terribly serious," I might say, or, "Each lady spoke an opinion and the others listened."

Or perhaps I should tell the whole truth? That I expected to remember what I had witnessed for the rest of my life.

"They were most complimentary about our pear tarts" is what I told Viola at supper.

MONDAY, OCTOBER 14

Alfred rode up the drive in the buggy as we came through the gate after school. His sombre face alerted us of dreadful news: Mrs. Goodhand's father, Horace Finchley, died late Saturday night.

Mr. Goodhand is packing a bag now and will go to be with his wife at the funeral in Berlin. Alfred is driving him to the evening train. Roy will be hired on to help on the farm for the three days until Mr. Goodhand returns. Poor

Alfred will sleep in the barn, as it would not be proper to have him under the same roof with Miss Viola Riley while both the Goodhands are away. Mrs. Campbell will travel with Mr. Goodhand, leaving her husband behind, and Elizabeth will stay with us starting tomorrow. All this was decided by Mr. Goodhand within minutes of the news.

The only person displaying any sorrow is Mrs. Campbell, and she is weeping enough for everyone. It's terribly sad that she did not travel to Berlin earlier, to bid her father farewell. Mr. Goodhand is a bully and she should have ignored him to do what she knew was right. She will feel regret for the rest of her life that she did not see her father on his deathbed.

Viola and I came up to our room as soon as our condolences were spoken. Of course we did not know Mrs. Goodhand's father and cannot pretend to grieve.

The upset in the kitchen was making me feel quite twitchy. I tried to read but could not settle my eyes upon the page. Viola poured water from the pitcher into the washbasin and began to scrub her hands.

"Viola?"

"Hmmm?"

"Do you remember the night when Father –"

"I remember."

She dried her hands and sat next to me on the bed.

"Remember how the sleet blew against the window?" said Viola. "And how Mama put on Father's robe against the cold?"

"But I didn't want you to keep the stove going," I said, "because Father wouldn't be there to split more wood."

"And then Mama said Arthur would do it now. From now on. It would be Arthur's job to look after us. Remember?"

"And we all cried."

Viola put her hand on top of mine, lying on the quilt. Her fingers were damp still from washing, cool and heavy. I did not move, not even a tremble, in case she pulled away.

But after a bit she stood up and tugged the towel straight on the washstand and corrected the placement of her brush and comb on the doily.

"I don't suppose it will do us good to venture backward," she said. "Mrs. Goodhand's trials are fresh and ours are grown over. It is she we must think on tonight."

I awoke in the dark from a dream where there was sleet again, hissing against the window. I suppose it was only chestnut branches. Viola was snoring, ever so gently. I'll have to tell her. I thought of Mrs. Goodhand's mother, spending the night alone after sharing her room for fifty-six years. Perhaps her husband snored like a bear. Will she cherish her first ever night of peace? Or will she toss and turn, aching for the buzzing drone that has been her lullaby for half a century?

Did my father snore? I don't remember. I could ask Mama.

Suddenly, I missed Mama with an ache I have not felt since we came to Sellerton. I tried to remember her face but could not. I tried to imagine her voice or her embrace but could not.

Then came a picture of her hands, folding bedsheets stiff from the clothesline. Her hands are brown and freckled, even in winter, her nails short and scrubbed clean. I could see them peeling apples, the way they do in October – hundreds of apples. Peeling, cutting, coring, slicing, picking up the next apple in her left hand, turning the paring knife in her right, the peelings coiling down to the newspaper on the floor, the white, naked apples going into the blue enamel basin with the chipped rim.

I felt better. Then I tried the same exercise with my father, which only baffled me again. I tried to picture the hands that held the Bible every night, but instead recalled the hard edge of the kitchen bench under my bottom while I wriggled, waiting for the passage to be done. I know he read aloud in a voice always gruff with a cough. I know he smacked his lips when he ate apple cake and left his boots under the table. But I know these qualities as I know a character in a story, because they are the details that my mother has repeated to us.

I do remember the sudden hole of not having him. The sound of my mother's leaky sniffling in the night; the discovery of his cap on its nail a month after he died; the charred tobacco in his pipe, sucked dry by his very own breath that was not breathing anymore.

I hugged my own arms for comfort. How odd that Mrs. Goodhand and Mrs. Campbell are tonight discovering the hole that I have felt since I was ten.

TUESDAY, OCTOBER 15

I wrote a condolence letter to Elizabeth about her grandfather, inking black the edge by hand as there were no mourning cards to be found about this house. I am not much practiced at this form of correspondence but did read the dozens Mama received upon my father's death. It seemed a wasted penny to post it, so I handed the envelope to Elizabeth as we lined up to make our manners at the morning's start.

At lunch, we sat together as has become our custom. (Whoever would have guessed it?) Elizabeth said that she has only met with her grandparents rarely and feels no sorrow on her own behalf. "But my mother grieves as if her heart has broken," she told me, "though never did a day go by while he lived that she did not complain of his lack of interest in her endeavors. Not that she endeavored to be more than a farm wife, and why should that interest him?"

WEDNESDAY, OCTOBER 16

We had a picnic for supper tonight! On the kitchen floor, the three of us girls. Viola scrambled eggs while Elizabeth and I toasted bread on forks over the fire. Roy and Alfred turned up late after milking, and we made the same again for them.

When they'd been fed, Roy suggested that since we used the floor for eating, we should use the table to play the new game that is so popular. We cleared away the cloth and centerpiece, and he took a small ball of string from his pocket. Roy said there are real balls and paddles manufactured to play, but home devices work near as well. The game was called Gossima until recently when it was changed to Ping-Pong, which sounds much more like a game, does it not? We had no paddles but used Mrs. Goodhand's smallest fry pans instead. The object of the game is to bounce the little ball back and forth across the table between two players without losing it to the floor. We got quite wild taking turns, until Viola remarked that we should perhaps not be so hilarious, this being a house of mourning.

One further footnote: Roy said he'd seen Mrs. Rattle walking home from the factory. She'd had a puncture and had to push the bicycle more than two miles. He helped her patch it so that she could ride to work in the morning.

"Did she mention me?" I asked. "Does she know you're working here?"

"No," said Roy.

Does she miss me? I wonder.

THURSDAY, OCTOBER 17

Alfred, Viola, Elizabeth, and I walked to the crossroads with Mrs. Watson after Endeavor this evening, just as we did three weeks ago. What a changed view I have of her now! (And not only because her belly is growing as the baby's time comes near.) Viola, of course, had no cause for an altered opinion and was perhaps warmer than before.

"It was a treat, Mable, to have you at our meeting on Sunday," said Mrs. Watson, as calm as you please. "Perhaps you'll bring along your sister next time."

"I found it most enlightening," I ventured. "I hope you found an answer to the worries of your special guests."

"We have a few ideas." Then off she went with a cheery little wave!

"That is one woman who will shortly have no time for reading," said Viola.

The Goodhands had arrived home while we were out, but Mrs. was already retired to her room.

"I'm glad you're here," said Mr. Goodhand. "Hazel's wanting some tea. She's all done in from the traveling."

Viola and I made up a tray: a pot of tea and bread and butter with a sprinkle of brown sugar. When I took it in to her, Mrs. Goodhand sat up in her bed looking dreadful, with her spectacles off and gray hair hanging limply about her shoulders. Of course, I've never seen it down before so it gave me a jolt. I tried to notice if she'd been crying, but I think she was just plain tired.

"Thank you, dearie," she said, patting the quilt for me to put the tray there. "Will you girls manage in the morning if I have a bit of a lie-in?"

"Oh, yes, Mrs. Goodhand. You take your rest." When I reached the door, I realized I should say something more. "I'm sorry about your father. I know it's a terrible loss."

Her eyes were closed but she nodded to show she'd heard.

FRIDAY, OCTOBER 18

I assembled the Commas at lunchtime, on the sunniest patch in the yard, and made them each recite the spelling list between bites of bread and cheese. Cathy whined and

Joseph glared mutinously, but all were word perfect for the bee! Unfortunately, Elizabeth took notice of our practice and performed the same, resulting in not quite the same triumph – Henry erred on *fascinate*.

Hiccuping Hyphens: 97

Celebrating Commas: 96

SATURDAY, OCTOBER 19

I cannot decide whether to go to Silver Lining tomorrow or not. (Will I even be welcome? Did I offend by leaving last week without saying goodbye? Or did she even notice? Am I simply a coward?)

I am still all of a jumble about what happened there.

"Will you listen to this," said Mr. Goodhand, reading the *Daily Beacon* as we readied the table for supper.

"KOREA'S NEW EMPRESS

The emperor of Korea has invited the foreign representatives to an entertainment to be given on October 23, when Lady Om will be introduced as the new empress. Lady Om was a slave girl rescued from captured pirates by the Korean court."

"Think of that!" said Mrs. Goodhand. "That's rather romantic, is it not?"

"Romantic? Humph!" said Mr. Goodhand. "What kind of a name is Om? Lady Om?"

"It's a Korean name, Dad," said Alfred. "In Korea they would think Howard to be a very odd name."

"Well, I don't go around putting my name in their newspapers, do I?" said Mr. Goodhand.

"It's quite a journey," said Viola, "from captured slave girl to empress."

"Better than the other way around," I said. "I would rather travel from slave to empress than from rich to poor like Mrs. Rattle. She grew up in a wealthy family but now is working in a factory!"

I received stares from all around the table.

"Mable," said Viola in her tight voice.

"It is not for us to say," said Mrs. Goodhand.

"I won't have gossiping here," said Mr. Goodhand.

"It's not gossip. She told me herself."

"I won't have backtalk, either."

"I wonder if Om will be a better empress because she has been oppressed and downtrodden before becoming rich?" I said.

Mr. Goodhand gave me a long look. "Could be you're spending too much time over there with that crackbrain," he warned.

We bent our heads and said grace. Supper was horrible. Mrs. Goodhand is back in the kitchen!

SUNDAY, OCTOBER 20

I was almost relieved to wake and find rain slashing the window. It made not going to visit Mrs. Rattle seem not quite of my own doing. She will look outside and think, *Oh, I suppose Mable did not come because of the rain.* Instead of *Oh, I suppose Mable did not come because she thinks I'm a crackbrain.*

Is she a crackbrain? Are all suffragists crackbrains? Or do they speak a truth the rest of us are not yet ready to live with? I cannot stop thinking about it. In the classroom this week, I looked at the little first-reader girls and wondered, Will they someday vote for the prime minister? Will one of them perhaps even *be* the prime minister? (Very doubtful, as Irene is rather silly and Ellen much too bossy for anyone to want her in charge.)

The rain did not prevent us from going to church, of course. The sermon was "Is God Tired?" I don't know about God, but I felt very tired myself to-day. I lay on our bed and read all afternoon – *Treasure Island* by Robert Louis Stevenson. It's a lovely adventure, full of frights. I wish I could put some beastly pirates into my romantic novel, but Helena is nowhere near the sea. Hattie will have to be satisfied with train bandits instead.

TUESDAY, OCTOBER 22

Cathy Forrest announced that her mother has bought her a new store dress for the Harvest Social on Saturday. Several others said their mothers are busily sewing. Elizabeth said she won't have anything new this year because the family is in mourning. Tommy Thomas said his mother is making nine angel food cakes for the refreshments table. Irene Singer swears that her father is providing Coca-Cola for everyone at the Social.

There will be a fiddler, but no dancing, of course. I understand why God might think dancing is too intimate an activity for public occasions, but I admit also to feeling the music in my feet sometimes and wishing to sway about. One day, when I'm *certain* God is busy – with a dreadful war somewhere – I would like to dance with a boy. We will have promenades at the Social, which are for the couples who are courting, or hoping to court. Would the Brown boys dare? I might have to do with Tommy Thomas, who is turning out to be more fun for the most part.

Part the Eighth
{Helena Is Abducted}

Our heroine blinked, seeing double. The train bandit, Captain Joseph Brigand, and his twin brother, Harry, were amused at her bewilderment. Suddenly, from the railway carriage behind her came a gunshot and gruff shouts.

Harry instantly signaled a boy, who held their horses nearby.

"Do excuse us," said Joseph, bowing to Helena. The brothers jumped astride their mounts and cantered toward the train, where a drama was unfolding!

The two men plundering the treasury carriage had encountered unexpected resistance from one of the guards. Although several heavy sacks lay in snowbanks beside the train, the courageous guard struggled to prevent a metal safe from being heaved overboard as well. It was he who had fired the shot, lodging a bullet in the chest of one of the criminals. Helena shuddered to see scarlet blood staining the snow beneath the wounded man, but watched agog as the twin bandits easily disarmed the guard and bound him tightly.

"Frederick!" called Harry to the boy. "Bring the horses!"

"Men!" shouted Joseph. "We're away!"

A burst of activity consumed the next minute. The loot was strapped to the snorting horses. Whiphand Pete emerged from the passenger car, pulling an iron bar across the doorway before he mounted his animal. The injured fellow was lifted into his saddle and joined there by the fifth bandit, who gripped him to prevent his sliding off in a faint.

Helena was frozen where she stood – in part by the winter wind but mainly in alarm and awe. As the laden horses thundered back toward her, Helena's only thought was a prayer that she not be crushed beneath their hooves. In the next moment, her heart jumped as strong arms embraced and then dragged her up upon the back of a galloping horse.

Helena, near swooning, held on to the man who now gazed into her green eyes.

"Our lad, Tom, is shot," said Joseph. "We need a nurse. You're coming with us."

To be continued . . .

(The Commas and the Hyphens are exactly at a draw!!)

Mr. Goodhand got as far as the "Letters to the Editor" tonight. Viola and I tidied the kitchen after supper while Mrs. Goodhand mixed the dough for tomorrow's bread.

"Will you listen to this? This beats all," he said.

"To the Editor,

How is it possible that here in the bucolic heart of Perth County there exists a place of such an unwholesome nature that it would more likely be discovered in the slums of Toronto?

A place where young women arrive in the darkness of dawn, return home in the darkness of evening, and toil in the dim light provided by a miserly master for the long hours in between?

A place where young women are forced to perform tedious tasks for twelve hours at a stretch with only two short breaks? A place where aching backs, blistered hands, strained eyes, and sore arms are the daily badges of being employed?

The place I speak of is central to the community of Stratford-Sellerton, and yet I doubt that anyone who has not visited within its walls is aware of its true character.

I speak of the Bright Creek Cheese Company, owned by Mr. Francis Forrest."

"Oh, mercy!" exclaimed Mrs. Goodhand, her floury hand on her mouth.

"There's more," said her husband. "You just wait."

Oh, double mercy, I thought. Mrs. Rattle is the bravest person I ever have met.

"To the outside world, Bright Creek is the familiar home of the Forrest family business, making and selling cheddar cheese for three generations. But inside its walls, Bright Creek keeps secrets, which are ugly to behold.

The women who make the cheese so cheerfully eaten at nearly every table in the county are afraid to speak the truth for fear of losing their jobs.

They suffer daily hours of hardship, stirring the curds with heavy long-handled rakes or scrubbing milk cans with scalding water. They tolerate the lewd remarks of the foreman or the insults of Mr. Forrest himself. They swallow the injustice of being fined for being moments late or speaking to a fellow slave during the endless day, and then opening a weekly pay packet of less than two dollars because the fines have been taken out."

"Is this all true?" asked Mrs. Goodhand.

"There's more yet," said Mr. Goodhand, continuing.

"These admirable women are not asking for charity. They are working to support themselves and their children. But they are asking questions. Such as, What sort of man drives a fancy carriage to church and dresses his wife in a fur cloak but takes money back from his workers for minor infractions?

And what sort of woman enjoys the riches wrung from the anguish of her sisters? Who ignores their plight instead of standing up to shout to the world that the time has come for change?

Look hard at your neighbours and ask yourselves fairly: Is this the world we wish to live in? Is this the example we wish to set for our children?

When will women have a voice on their own behalf? And when that time comes, will you be able to look them in the eye and say you support them?

Sincerely,

A Good Neighbour"

"Whoever has written this?" said Mrs. Goodhand. She punched the bread dough with vigour.

"It takes brazen stupidity to publish something like this," said Mr. Goodhand. "The Forrests might be understood for committing murder."

I felt Alfred's eyes upon me. I caught his glance and looked away. He remembered the day at the post office when she had announced her new job. There was a look exchanged between Alfred and my sister.

"I think," said Viola slowly, "I think I am correct in believing the author to be Mrs. Rattle. Am I right, Mable?"

I knew not where to look. I was hot from my skull to my toenails. The Goodhands stared. Viola tilted her head, watching me.

"I cannot claim to know it as a fact," I said. I dreaded their remarks, thinking I would be held responsible for Mrs. Rattle's action.

"Humph," said Mr. Goodhand. "She's a sneaky one but clever, I'll give her that. I wouldn't be in Forrest's shoes tonight, no sir!"

"I never saw you as one to support emancipation, Dad," said Alfred.

"I don't," said Mr. Goodhand. "Flat out, women are built to look after things in a home. But if what the newspaper says is true, there's no call to be treating people this way.

Look at cows. You have to treat them with respect if you want them to produce good milk. They need fresh air and sweet hay and plenty of time to digest. If you overwork a cow, you've tossed away your own cream. That's just foolish."

"Dad," Alfred said, grinning, "that might be the smartest thing you ever said."

"Doesn't mean women aren't better off as wives," said Mr. Goodhand. "But some of them are widows or haven't found a husband yet. They've got a living to make, too. They don't need to be mistreated by a self-important bully like Francis Forrest. He was that way in school, and I didn't like him then. He must be madder than a kicked dog, being attacked by a woman."

"That may be, Howard," said Mrs. Goodhand. "But Bright Creek buys our milk. If this woman makes trouble at the factory, it's our livelihood that's put in danger. You'd best keep that in mind."

"Mable?" said Viola. "I warned you before and I repeat the warning: You stay away from her."

"Mmmm," I said.

Mrs. Goodhand gave me a sharp look and lay the tea cloths over the rising bread.

It is a large hornet indeed that Mrs. Rattle has released into the pantry.

SUNDAY, OCTOBER 27 - THE HARVEST SOCIAL

Where to begin with my record of the Harvest Social? I hope I can write it all down quickly before I forget a single detail!

Elizabeth arrived after luncheon yesterday so that we could begin our preparations early. It was much jollier to have her there than to be alone with Viola.

"Did you know?" she whispered as we hurried to the bedroom. "Did you know from Mrs. Rattle that she was planning to provoke a scandal?"

For a moment I was tempted to pretend, to say yes, that Mrs. Rattle trusted me enough to have confided all her plans. . . .

I shook my head.

"Oh, well," said Elizabeth – disappointed, I could see. "I was hoping for some news from the inside. Isn't this just the most delicious disaster?"

"Elizabeth?" Viola appeared behind us on the stair.

"Yes, Miss Riley?"

"The subject of Mrs. Rattle is forbidden in this household."

"Yes, Miss Riley."

We took turns washing hair, using the iron, trying on dresses, choosing ribbons, changing our minds, and so on. Viola eventually relented from her schoolmarm mood and joined the fun. She was kind enough to lend me her pale green shirtwaist, which almost fits and felt almost new. She wore the gray, which is so elegant. Alfred used pomade to slick down his hair. He clearly thought he was debonair, but I prefer his regular floppy red curls.

We all squeezed into the buggy for Alfred to drive us to the church hall. I felt quite sorry for Darling hauling such a load, but not sorry enough to climb down and walk. I was too excited to get there using shank's pony!

We came into the hall, shed our cloaks, and were swept up in the circle of girls, admiring each others' dresses. Cathy Forrest strutted back and forth in a blue velvet with ribbon trim. I shall be catty and say it is much too nice a dress for such a brat to wear. Viola looked a bit lost (not having, as yet, made any friends in Sellerton), but I saw her later with Mrs. Watson, so she wasn't completely alone. I did not see the Brown boys. Elizabeth and I made our escape to the refreshments and were followed by Tommy Thomas and his little sister, Lyddie.

Mrs. Forrest was at the cake and pie table, arranging name cards for the entries in the baking contest. She wore a new hat, which looked as though a naughty boy hiding up a tree had dropped a bird's nest on her head, complete with a fat robin peering over the brim.

"And that's the mister," whispered Elizabeth, pointing to a man lurking nearby, holding tightly to his sons hand.

It was my first sight of Mr. Forrest, and he looked nothing like a villain. I'd been hoping for a whip and a spiky mustache, but he was an undersized man with sloping shoulders and a red face.

"I wouldn't dare go to a Social if I knew everyone would be talking about me," said Elizabeth.

"Just think of him snoring," I whispered back, "like a dinosaur."

We had to cover our mouths for laughing. Viola shot us a look from across the room.

"I'm hungry," said Lyddie, eyeing the feast spread out before us. (It would take two pages to list all the offerings. Suffice to say, no one went hungry!) We filled our plates and found Joseph and Henry already eating, so we shared a table with them.

When the plates were finally stacked and the tables tidied, we prepared for the next portion of the evening. Reverend Scott stood behind the lectern, picking crumbs of angel food cake from his beard. Finally, he called the room to order and announced the first promenade.

The Ladies Committee had ruled that no one younger than high school could participate in the promenades, so our group hugged the wall as spectators. We had a good view and much to say about all the dresses.

"Choose a partner, gentlemen," advised Reverend Scott. "We will begin shortly. After three circuits of the hall, you may exchange partners and start again."

There was a flurry of cosmetic adjustment among the young women: hair patting, cheek pinching, lip rolling, skirt smoothing, until the young men inched forward to make their selection. I was pleased to see Alfred bowing like a prince in front of Viola.

"The topic for our first promenade," said Reverend Scott, "to be discussed by our young people: 'Is It Better to Be Clever or Good?' What will they have to say about that, eh? Let the walk begin!" And off they went in a stately stroll, as if they were taking the air in the Palace Gardens.

Roy asked Viola for the second promenade. The topic was "What I Should Like to Have Said about Me."

"I'd like you to say that I'm clever and beautiful," Elizabeth informed us.

"No chance of that," said Henry Brown.

Elizabeth pretended to swat him and turned to me. "What about you, Mable?"

"It's a difficult question," I said, "if we're to pick only one thing."

"I think we can all agree that I'm handsome," said Joseph.

"No," said Henry. "I'm the handsome one." We all laughed.

"I'd like Mama to think I'm good," said Lyddie, "even if I'm not."

"Maybe if you stop swiping spoonfuls of jam from the fruit cellar," said Tommy.

"I know," I said. "I think most I'd like to be brave."

We were all making things up and laughing when there fell a hush in the room. We looked around, thinking the second promenade was done and the partners switching. But it was a new arrival who had caused the quiet. Mrs. Rattle stood just inside the doorway, wearing a skirt and a hat! She looked splendid all dressed up.

Perhaps the Ladies Reading Circle had planned that Miss Robertson should step forward to meet her.

"Good evening," fluttered Miss Robertson. "You've missed the supper, but I'm sure we can rustle you up some dessert if you're inclined. Isn't it nice to greet a new parishioner, Reverend Scott?"

"Well, now," said the reverend, looking confused. "Yes, indeed."

"Come with me, Mrs. Rattle." Miss Robertson led her gently aside as Reverend Scott signaled the fiddler to recommence his promenade accompaniment. The couples began again to walk and chat under the minister's watchful eye.

I slid along the wall toward the food table. I suspect that Mrs. Rattle had no wish for a lemon curd tart, but she took the plate from Miss Robertson and nodded graciously. She no doubt realized that many eyes were still directed her way and that Mrs. Forrest paced like a panther behind the rows of cakes and pies.

Mrs. Forrest did not try to hide her displeasure at Mrs. Rattle's appearance. These were Mrs. Forrest's friends, after all. Her church, her Harvest Social, her pumpkin pies. It could not seem right that someone who had insulted her in the newspaper should march in and make her feel discomfited in her own beehive.

I gathered my nerve and crept hurriedly over to speak with Mrs. Rattle.

"Why have you come here?" I pleaded quietly, looking into her eyes. "Don't you realize you've caused dreadful upset?"

"Mable Riley." She laid a hand upon my shoulder, balancing her tart plate in the other. "That was exactly my intention. I am ready for upset. I crave upset. Only upset leads to change."

Her eyes shifted, watching someone behind me. I turned to see Mrs. Forrest squinting at us.

Miss Robertson jumped in. "Mrs. Rattle will need a fork for her tart," she said loudly.

"Oh, no," said Mrs. Forrest. "She's not to be trusted with a fork, that one. There's no telling who she might stab in the back if we give her a fork."

"I'll use my fingers," said Mrs. Rattle. "After all, they work well enough to type my letters." She bit into the rim of her pastry.

The anger blazed in Mrs. Forrest's eyes, but as she opened her mouth to retort, her husband smacked his hand upon the table next to us, making the platters and doilies jump.

"I don't know how you make your peace with God," he growled at Mrs. Rattle. "To stir up trouble as you have done and then to come here and make jokes?"

His voice increased in volume as his fury caught fire. The halfhearted promenade trailed to nothing as this new entertainment commanded attention.

"I'm a hard-working man," said Mr. Forrest. "I hire inexperienced girls, like yourself, and give them a place to earn their keep. If I make mistakes, well, I'm human. But for you to go about slandering my good name . . . That's ungrateful and downright criminal." He shook his fist at her. "And if your type is welcome in this hall, then I'm in the wrong place!"

He took a step toward the door but then remembered his wife.

"Are you with me, Mrs. Forrest?" He looked around, his red face shining redder.

"Oh, no, Mr. Forrest," said his wife. She came out from behind the table, pulling off her apron as if preparing for a school-yard fight. "It will take a snowstorm in July to chase me out of a room I want to be in. I am the chair of the Ladies Church Committee, and I have something to say to this lying hussy."

She waddled forward, adjusting her silly hat. When she stood only a yard away, she spoke again, spraying as the words flew out in anger.

"How dare you push your nose in where it doesn't belong! This is the way you repay Mr. Forrest for the kindness of hiring you? With slurs and slander? You are not wanted in Sellerton. You can just take your bicycle and your fancy britches and be gone!"

Mrs. Rattle stayed still and inhaled slowly, remarkably cool in the face of such an assault.

"I have only reported what I experienced firsthand in your husband's factory, Mrs. Forrest. His business will benefit from improving conditions for the women who work there. Ignoring the problem will cause great unrest. Your workers *and* the quality of your cheese will suffer."

"Are you threatening me, you saucy chit?"

"I am stating fact, madam."

"You're not worth the time it took to train you!" shouted Mr. Forrest. "We don't need your kind at Bright Creek. Your employ is terminated as of this minute!"

"I would be very much disappointed if that were *not* the case," said Mrs. Rattle. Her voice was quiet, but it carried to the corners of the room. No one had expected such a drama at the Harvest Social and everyone listened eagerly.

I believe it was my own admiring smile that set Mrs. Forrest off on her next fury. "Miss Riley?" She swung her glare to Viola, who had inched closer to us. "The fact that you permit your sister to consort with this monster is an indication of your poor moral standards."

Viola's cheeks burned pink. Her fingers curled into fists, but she pinched her lips together. How could she stay silent? She no doubt imagined the end of her own employ if she were to defend herself.

I felt Mrs. Rattle's gaze upon me. Had I not just claimed a wish for bravery? This was surely my chance to shine.

"Excuse me," I said, my palms damp. "My sister is not responsible for my friendships. I may speak with whomever I please. Mrs. Rattle is the most admirable lady I have ever met, and I believe every word she wrote in the newspaper."

I might have continued, but Alfred quickly shuffled me toward the door. I heard Mrs. Rattle thank me but did not witness anything more. Viola and the Goodhands departed in a cluster around me, and we hurried to where Darling was patiently waiting.

"Well, I never," Mrs. Goodhand kept murmuring. "I never did."

"That was an impressive confrontation," said Alfred. "I shouldn't like to cross Mrs. Rattle. She makes a formidable foe."

He winked at me, but Viola shivered.

"I do not like to scold you in front of others, Mable," she began. "But your behaviour this evening has shamed the Goodhands and very likely put an end to my position at Sellerton School." Her voice broke in anguish. "You are quite the most selfish, thoughtless —"

"Now, now." Mr. Goodhand interrupted Viola's tirade by patting her arm with a big paw. "I don't feel shamed," he said. "I do not approve of your sister's manners, but nobody thinks I reared her."

He turned to me. "In fact, I aim to thank you. That was quite the shortest Social I've ever had to endure." And then he began to chuckle, wheezing with the unused effort of it.

Viola stared at him, aghast. Alfred burst out laughing, and Mrs. Goodhand kept muttering as if she hadn't heard at all.

So, that was the Social!

How did I dare? I awoke many times during this night wondering, How did I dare? Then I thought of Mrs. Forrest's snarling mouth and felt a flush of victory that I looked straight at her quivering chins and spoke my mind!

MONDAY, OCTOBER 28

Viola said not a word on the way to school. Happily, we met up with Elizabeth at the turn, so I had a companion. Viola strode ahead while Elizabeth and I slowed our pace to discuss Saturday evening once again.

It was not until we reached the schoolhouse that I discovered the further-reaching effects of my outburst. Most scholars refused to look at me straight or to speak with me. It was as if I were wearing a sign pinned to my back saying AVOID ME. The Brown boys turned away in the cloakroom instead of pushing me back and forth in their teasing way.

Cathy and Frank Forrest were kept home. The rumour is that their mother won't let them come to school so long as Miss Riley is teacher. There were several other scholars absent as well, but we cannot be certain it's me to blame.

Elizabeth listened in to what the others were whispering. "They merely repeat what their parents have told them," she reported. "They say you've been infected by the wicked Mrs. Rattle. Infected or enchanted, depending on who is speaking. The question is whether you will first bring harm to yourself or to the Goodhands."

I know my cheeks were hot, but I know not which caused the hotter flame: shame or anger. I was sorry to cause distress to the Goodhand household, but it irked me to be shunned.

Elizabeth sat quietly at my side while we ate lunch sheltered from the wind behind the schoolhouse. Tommy suddenly plunked himself down, with his usual toothy grin.

"Well, Mable," he said, "the classroom is certainly quiet to-day, with no one talking to you. You no doubt please your sister in your muffled condition."

"Aren't you saucy, Tommy Thomas," said Elizabeth. "It's not Mable's choice to be ignored."

"Did you not choose to defy Mrs. Forrest?" Tommy asked me.

"Well, yes. But I supposed that my schoolmates would cheer me on."

"I did, Mable. It was a treat. I'd spend my allowance to see it again."

I kicked him.

"Really!" He dodged me and went on. "But two of your schoolmates bear the name of Forrest. Did you expect them to cheer your betrayal of their mother? Or their friends? Or their friends' families?"

"I had not considered that."

Elizabeth giggled. "Not that Cathy Forrest has too many friends."

"True enough," said Tommy. He winged his apple core at a squirrel, who dashed along the fence top.

And I puzzled over the matter of loyalty and betrayal. Who had I betrayed? Mrs. Forrest or the Goodhands? And to whom was I loyal? Mrs. Rattle or myself?

Mr. Goodhand was in high spirits this evening, reading the newspaper.

"PERSONAL AND SOCIAL NOTES
The Sellerton Harvest Social was held Saturday
night at the Methodist Church hall. The Ladies
Church Committee provided a fine spread, under
the leadership of Mrs. Francis Forrest, who also
baked the prize-winning pumpkin pie."

"It doesn't mention she was also the judge," sniffed Mrs. Goodhand.

"There were six promenades, each with a topic of
great interest to the young folk attending.

"They stuck around for six, eh? And we got away after only two!" Mr. Goodhand's chuckle creaked again.

"The festivities were punctuated by a lively discussion among several prominent members of the community.

"Lively discussion?" said Mr. Goodhand. "That's what you call it, eh?"

"Dad, if this doesn't show you that newspapers report only part of the story, I don't know what will," said Alfred.

As I readied for bed tonight, I thought about my situation. I have had a taste of being an outcast and do not like the flavour. It makes me more sympathetic than ever to Mrs. Rattle's lonely place outside. She suffers only because she says what she believes to be true. We are taught that honesty is honourable and that to tell a lie is to sin. But the payment for speaking the truth aloud is this awful shunning. How difficult it is to make the right choice!

TUESDAY, OCTOBER 29

School was not quite so lonely to-day. Tommy and Elizabeth ate lunch with me again, but we were joined by the Browns and Rachel from Grade Five. Adeline, the Mennonite girl, who neither knows nor cares about Socials or suffragists, was happy to have me for a reading partner. And my little first-years were ready to slide their hands back into mine and pat my knees despite what their parents might be saying at home.

Mr. Goodhand did not read aloud the "Personal and Social Notes" this evening. He stopped on the front page.

"Will you listen to this," he said. "The brute has got his just rewards.

"CZOLGOSZ ELECTROCUTED
PRESIDENT MCKINLEY'S ASSASSIN
PAYS PENALTY OF HIS CRIME

Auburn, N.Y. Leon F. Czolgosz was executed in the death chamber of the state prison here at 7:42 this morning. He made but a brief speech before death. He said he was not sorry for what he had done but expressed regret that he had not seen his father."

The newspapers call electrocution the new "humane method" of execution. Is it humane to be sizzled like a sausage? I do not like to think about it. How does the father of Leon Czolgosz feel this evening? Is he regretful also? Did he love his son and forgive this terrible deed? Or is he relieved to wash his hands of the young man who brought shame to the family name?

THURSDAY, OCTOBER 31

I stayed home from Endeavor this evening. Viola urged me to go. "Take every opportunity to seek God's forgiveness," she said, but I simply could not bear the church ladies' scorn. I helped Mrs. Goodhand with the mending instead, which was just as dreary. All the household is concerned that "Mable be well occupied" so that I am not tempted by irreverence. . . .

PART THE NINTH
{IN THE VILLAIN'S DEN}

Helena awoke to find herself surrounded by her abductors in the warm kitchen of a humble farmhouse. Captain Brigand pressed a flask of brandy to her lips, forcing the burning liquid to spark her wits to clarity. "We have no time to nurse the nurse," he explained. "Do what you can for our Tom."

Helena turned to the wounded man, laid out upon a wooden bench. She realized at once that Tom was but a frightened boy, scarcely older than she.

She requested a blanket, boiled water, and a linen sheet cut into strips for bandages. Then Helena gently pulled away Tom's shirt, soaked with blood. The bullet had missed his heart, for the hole was somewhat lower on his chest. He flinched as her fingers probed the spot to discover that indeed the bullet was within him still and lodged between two ribs.

"He'll need brandy," said Helena.

Joseph understood. He urged Tom to swallow several times. Helena worked swiftly; slipping her fingers beneath the flesh, she seized the bullet and pulled it sharply out of its trap.

Tom uttered a cry and then fainted dead away. She cleansed the tear again and wrapped it carefully, knowing she had done her best.

"I am not a real nurse," Helena reminded the men. "You must find a doctor to dress the wound properly."

"We have no doctor hereabouts to trust," said Harry gruffly, touching the scar upon his own cheek.

"Send a fellow for some salve, at least," she pleaded. "And be sure to change the dressing twice each day."

"You'll be here to do that for him," said Harry. "We cannot release you now."

Helena bowed her head in an effort to smother her dismay.

While the brothers conferred with their compatriots in the next room, Helena hurried to the window, hoping to discover other dwellings nearby. Alas, the farm was on a hillside with no evidence of humanity in sight.

"Feather will go," said Joseph, entering the kitchen with their fifth man at his side. "Tell him what you'll need to prepare our supper, too."

Helena laughed. "Surely you do not think I am a cook as well as a nurse?" she said. "Who has cooked for you until now?"

"Young Tom."

Helena laughed again. "It is your misfortune that you abducted an earl's daughter," she said. "There is truth in the saying that a rich woman is a useless one. I have always had servants. I do not know how to cook."

At that moment, poor Tom whimpered in his sleep and Helena's heart turned over. She realized he would need sustenance if he was to heal.

"Ask the butcher for bones," she told Feather. "Perhaps together we can make a soup."

And indeed, several hours later, the men had feasted on a rustic soup, bread, and cheese. Tom had revived enough to join the banter and to grasp his nurse's hand in thanks.

'Twas past midnight before the house was quiet and the men at rest. Helena had volunteered to sit beside the patient in case he should need her. He appeared to sleep soundly, however, and she knew he would make a full recovery if the bandits continued the treatment as she had instructed them.

Quietly, she tied her green velvet traveling cape about her neck, noticing how worn it looked after only twenty-four hours of adventure. As she stepped outside, she rejoiced in the clear night and looked to the stars for guidance on the next leg of her journey.

Before two minutes' walking, however, there came a shout. She turned to see Tom, waving from the doorway. He hobbled after her, wearing no shirt, his bandages lit by the moon.

"Please!" he called. "Come back!"

Helena thought she could outrun him, but as she watched, Tom stumbled and fell to the ground, where he lay unmoving.

To be continued . . .

FRIDAY, NOVEMBER 1

Such a naughty thing I did this afternoon. I learned a trick; during the turn of a Hapless Hyphen to spell, I would grimace suddenly, as if wincing in sympathy at an error made, and thus rattle the speller's concentration and provoke the very error I wished for! I dared not overdo the operation for fear of being noticed, but the Cheering Commas are now leading the race!

As soon as I was home from school, Mrs. Goodhand found work for me.

"We have run low on butter," she said, and gave me a quart-sized pickling jar full of milk that I might make enough butter to carry us through supper and breakfast. I took it outdoors, thinking to watch twilight descend while I tizzied the jar.

So there I was, shaking about at the garden gate like a girl with fits, and who should happen by on his bicycle?

Tommy Thomas! I must have turned the colour of a stewed tomato. Though I stood rigid in an instant, it took me a full minute to find my tongue.

"Why, Tommy!" (As close to squealing as a trapped mouse). "Where might you be going?"

He peered at me through those bent-up spectacles and then grinned.

"I heard there was a dancing show at the Goodhand farm," he said. "I came early for a front-row seat."

"Oh, you!" I pretended to clunk him with the jar of nearly butter.

He had brought his new birthday copy of the *Wonderful Wizard of Oz* to exchange for my *Treasure Island*, which I have been performing to much acclaim at lunch recess.

When my milk was transformed, I quickly poured off the buttermilk and rinsed the butter. I added a trickle of carrot juice for colour and served Tommy one of Viola's biscuits smothered in minute-old butter before sending him on his way. I pray the taste erased the sight of me making it!

SATURDAY, NOVEMBER 2

"Mother," said Alfred after luncheon, "you've had a difficult time of things and you look a bit peaked. I'm sure

Viola wouldn't mind cooking the supper this once. Mable could help. Wouldn't that be a good way to keep her out of trouble?"

Mrs. Goodhand looked us over as if we had just met.

"Well, it might be nice at that, to be treated like a lady in my own home."

"Have yourself a lazy afternoon," said Alfred.

"There's a chicken waiting," Mrs. Goodhand told Viola. "You know where to find the potatoes."

Alfred winked at me and patted his stomach.

"I've been craving your sister's roast chicken with giblet gravy," he whispered as his mother left the room.

SUNDAY, NOVEMBER 3

Another Sunday gone and I did not visit Silver Lining.

"It's best that you stay home," said Viola. "Nothing good has come from her direction yet."

The sad truth is, I do not *want* to go there. Am I a shivering coward? I cannot bring myself to seek out certain trouble.

Viola thinks I'm sulking, but it's not so simple as that. I am forlorn and thwarted. Like holding a pitcher full of feelings and having nowhere to pour.

I could not wait until Sunday. From school I walked to Mrs. Rattle's cottage despite having to carry my satchel full of books and spelling papers. It was dusk by the time I knocked upon her door.

"Mable Riley! How good to see you! I'm so glad you haven't been frightened off forever. Do come in. We are having an emergency meeting of the, er, Reading Circle." She laughed and led me into the parlour, where Mrs. Watson and Miss Thomas were seated by the fire.

"Is it wise to have the child here?" asked Miss Thomas.

"She has shown us where her heart lies, has she not?" said Mrs. Rattle.

My heart, though, was heavy. On my journey there, I had imagined for us a reunion of great warmth, perhaps even giddiness. I had pictured us in an embrace of tearful rejoicing. We would drink lemonade out of crystal glasses and pop corn over the fire. I had forgotten she is a woman occupied with serious matters. She has no time for school-girl fancies. Thankfully, she could not read my mind and would not suspect my foolishness. I blush to think!

I bid myself to sit and pay attention to the conversation. And what should I discover but a plot for rebellion against the Bright Creek Cheese Company.

"There has recently been a strike at the Penning garment factory in Toronto, where the girls were going blind from sewing in bad light every day for twelve or fourteen hours," explained Miss Thomas. "They stopped work for over two weeks, and finally the foreman agreed to hear their points."

"Francis Forrest will not be expecting a rebellion from his brow-beaten girls," Mrs. Rattle was saying. "We will have the advantage of surprise at least."

My face must have expressed some of the distress I felt.

"Mable, you look as though you have something to say."

"You may not want to hear it," I said. "I know your complaints are justified, but my sister and I are boarders on the Goodhand farm. They have twenty cows and they sell their milk to Bright Creek." I took a breath and rushed on. "No one should have to work as hard for so little pay as the girls. But it's not the farmers who should be punished. The Goodhands depend on the Forrests' factory. If work is disrupted there, it is they who will suffer. The milk will sour and they will lose custom. The farmers will be angry, not sympathetic to your cause."

I had never said so much before. The ladies stared at me and then at one another.

"It's good you see more than one perspective, Mable Riley," said Mrs. Rattle. "That is a sign of a maturing mind. All that you say is true, though we hope to have the farmers' support once they understand the situation. Sometimes we must perform a small wrong in order to do a great right. That is our justification. We are working toward a very great right."

Ambler's Corners
November 7, 1901

Oh, Mable!

Quel scandale! How daring of you to cause a scene! Fancy entering a shouting match with a lady from the church committee! This is not the Mable I remember. Your sister must have wished to throttle you! Or drag you off to the doctor with suspicion of a brain fever! I hope you have recovered your reason by now and have returned to being the sensible Mable I know and love.

Though sensible does not describe your literary sketches, either! Where do you summon your ideas?! Our heroine digging out bullets and touching naked chests and whatever next?! Is your life catching up with your story or else the other way around?

Your spelling bees sound quite the entertainment.

Though you will not like me to say so, I think it might do you good to rely upon a team for your triumphs. There are times when humble pie should be digested. My news is quite tame. I received top marks in algebra (since you are not here to steal that spot) and a commendation for my report in French.

Jimmy Fender is carrying my books home from school each afternoon. There, I've told you! Please do not be jealous or try to win him back.

Your friend,
Hattie

P.S. If you smell this, do not imagine I have started to smoke. My brother put the writing paper into an empty cigar box my father has finished using.

I wish I had not told Hattie anything about the Harvest Social or Mrs. Rattle. She has made it all sound so sordid and silly. And as if I'd care about Jimmy Fender!

FRIDAY, NOVEMBER 8

Good news: Dottie Blau was ill to-day! And Cathy Forrest not present, of course, thanks to the evil lurking in Miss Riley's schoolhouse. The Commas maintained our (slight) lead. If I were wicked, I should feed Dottie a bowlful of castor oil next Thursday evening!

One of Tommy's words was *beautiful*, and he looked *right at me* while he spelled it (correctly)! I was certainly crimson-faced and dared not look his way again until dismissal. Poor Tommy would never win a blue ribbon for Best Looking, but he certainly is more clever and fun than anyone else.

PART THE TENTH
{THE TRUE MISSION}

Helena returned to the bandits' dwelling and cared for Tom throughout the night and the following day. He was fevered and raving, a condition brought on by his effort to prevent Helena from escaping.

She was a tender nurse, and when Tom recovered his senses, he was an obliging patient. From his sickbed, he instructed Feather how to prepare the evening meal of roast pork with onions and baked apples.

"Where did you learn to cook?" asked Helena in admiration as she dressed his wound after supper.

"It was my job at the orphanage," said Tom, "to help in the kitchen."

"Orphanage?" she inquired softly.

"Why, yes," said Tom. "That's where we all here became brothers. St. Jerome's Home for Foundlings."

Helena was propelled to her feet by the swell of pity in her heart. "What? This whole band of train robbers began as motherless waifs?"

"Indeed," said Tom. "'Tis the reason for our banditry as well as our bond. So great is our affection for the admirable woman who cared for us, Mama Tinker, that we are sworn to find the money she needs to carry on her good work."

"How can the work be good if it is financed by villainy? Is there no better way?"

"As we are uneducated ourselves, train robbery is our only path to the quantity of gold required to save the lives of countless children. Sometimes we must perform a small wrong in order to do a great right."

Helena was chastened by her mistaken judgment upon her hosts. Those she had thought to be fierce and greedy raiders were the kindest of men, motivated by gratitude to the loving woman who had raised a thousand children as her own.

"Most folks are thrilled to brag that they've been robbed," continued Tom with a laugh. "They give up their trinkets with no great sorrow in exchange for a tale to tell."

Helena thought briefly of her beloved moon-shaped brooch but then listened again to Tom as she wiped his brow with a cool cloth.

"Our trouble now," he whispered, "is that St. Jerome's has grown too small to hold all of the orphans. We must find and purchase a new home."

He closed his eyes.

"Hush now," soothed Helena, her calming tones working their magic for only a minute before a distant rumble disturbed the quiet. Shouts of warning came from the other room.

"Saddle up! Away, boys!" called Harry.

Helena heard Pete and Feather rush out the back door to the horses. She hurried to the window, to see uniformed men on horseback galloping toward their door.

"Can you ride, Tom?" asked Joe.

"He mustn't!" cried Helena.

"I will," said Tom, using his friend's arm for support as he stood.

"They're riding fast," said Harry from the window watch. "We may be caught unless we fight."

"No bloodshed," ordered Joe.

"I will walk out and distract the soldiers while you make your escape," cried Helena. "Go quickly! While you still have a chance!"

She pushed Harry toward the door. Her last view of Tom was of his pale face looking back over his shoulder at her.

Eight soldiers halted their steeds only a few yards from where Helena stood on the side porch, their eyes showing surprise at facing a woman.

"Greetings! How can I help you, gentlemen?" she called, trying to keep terror from colouring her voice. Every moment that she engaged them allowed her new comrades to escape a few feet farther away behind the cabin.

"We're hunting outlaws, ma'am," said the lieutenant gruffly. "We have reason to believe this farmhouse is a refuge for dangerous train bandits."

"Oh my!" said Helena.

"We'll have to ask you to stand aside so's we can take a look inside your house." The men swung down from their saddles, but Helena stayed planted a moment longer.

"Can I get you fellows anything to drink?" she asked with a saucy tilt of her head. "Hot lemon, perhaps? Or tea?"

The soldiers brushed past her and stomped up the porch steps.

To be continued . . .

WEDNESDAY, NOVEMBER 13

Viola will scold me for another candle gone, but I must record all that happened here this night.

We had company after supper. Viola spied her through the window and cleverly excused herself before the knock came. I was not so quick-witted and was requested by Mr. Goodhand to open the door. Mrs. Forrest looked straight past me and surveyed the room.

"Mrs. Goodhand," she said, ignoring the rest of us.

"Mrs. Forrest." Mrs. Goodhand's voice was chill. She wiped her hands on her apron.

"A word, if you will? On the porch?" Mrs. Forrest cupped a hand around her words, indicating she had secret business.

"Well, no, I'm not inclined to be sitting outdoors in this weather," said Mrs. Goodhand.

Mr. Goodhand scraped back his chair and stood up. "We'll leave you alone in here," he said. "I've got a pig to look at." He pulled his jacket from a hook and headed out to the barn, with Alfred at his heels.

That left me to be the thistle in her thumb. Mrs. Forrest pursed her lips.

"Please excuse me, Mrs. Goodhand," I said. "I need to go upstairs to prepare my lessons for tomorrow."

Mrs. Forrest snorted.

There came another knock upon the door and in came Elizabeth's mother, as she often does of an evening.

"It's good you're here, Mrs. Campbell," said Mrs. Forrest. "This concerns your daughter as well as my own children." She noticed me lingering by the newel post. "Go on, missy, up you go. You've no business here."

I clomped my feet upon the steps and down the hall-way to the door of our room, but crept back quickly to where I might overhear.

". . . should be replaced," Mrs. Forrest was saying, "before an incident occurs bearing grave consequences."

"Elizabeth has never shown as much interest in her lessons as she has this fall or scored so well," said Mrs. Campbell. "I have no objection to Miss Riley."

"I will not support the dismissal of the schoolmistress because of her sister's high spirits," said Mrs. Goodhand. "As misguided as Mable is at times, she is well intentioned. And Miss Riley has been most responsible in her efforts to control her. She is adamant that Mable no longer associate with the Widow Rattle, who worked for your husband. That way lies trouble."

"Don't talk to me about trouble," said Mrs. Forrest. "After all we've done for our hired hands, we never expected such ingratitude. But those indolent girls at the factory are about to learn the real meaning of trouble. They think they're so clever, with their pennants and their sign waving. Ha! We'll show them clever. There's nothing like a good conk on the head with a policeman's truncheon to know who's clever."

"Surely not, Suzanna!" Mrs. Campbell sounded shocked.

"They'd be showing good sense to wear iron bonnets tomorrow. I won't say more than that. . . ." Her ghastly laughter, even more than the threat of her words, sent chills straight down my backbone.

"Mable?" Viola was calling me. I tiptoed back to answer her and shortly heard the door below, signaling our guest's departure.

I readied to retire, pondering all the while the devout belief that Mrs. Forrest holds about her own generosity. How is it that a person can blind herself to truth? Or – and this is the frightening thought – is it Mrs. Rattle and the factory women who are blind? Is *everyone* blind to what they do not wish to see?

Normally, it would not be an adventure to walk out the kitchen door to visit a neighbour a mile along the road. But I have discovered that an adventure is anything that makes your heart beat faster, as mine certainly did tonight!

The Goodhands retired early, as they always do, by 9:15. Alfred and Viola remained chatting together for some time after, until finally I urged Viola to come help sponge the hem of my skirt. Then, while she was at the privy, I pulled my nightdress over my clothing and snuggled beneath the quilt, tucking my stockinged toes under me so that Viola should not glimpse them when she came to bed.

It seemed forever before Viola's breaths were steady enough to convince me that she slept. At long last, I crept from the bed, pulled off my nightdress, and collected my boots from beside the bureau.

The stairs creaked, the floor creaked, the door creaked – altogether enough creaking to send me into fits! I fumbled in the dark kitchen to tie my laces, listening above my thudding heart for wakeful Goodhands.

Outside, with a chilly wind at my back, I set out briskly for Silver Lining. I was relieved to find the house still alight when I arrived. Mrs. Rattle wore a look of alarm when she answered my knocking and smiled uneasily.

"Mable Riley! Whatever are you doing here? You must be frozen to the marrow. Come in at once!"

The parlour was warm, the fire burning. Mrs. Rattle's hair was plaited for bed and she wore a black sateen wrapper.

"Mrs. Rattle, please excuse my disturbing you. I am delivering urgent news."

"What is it?"

"Mrs. Forrest was a caller at the Goodhand farm this evening."

"I pity Mrs. Goodhand."

"She came to rally support to terminate my sister's contract."

"Dreadful woman."

"But, she spoke of a plan –"

"Yes?"

"She said there will be policemen at Bright Creek tomorrow, prepared to do battle! They've been instructed to beat the women if they insist on protesting."

Mrs. Rattle flinched. "How much lower can they sink?"

"She laughed," I told her. "Mrs. Forrest laughed and said the girls should wear iron bonnets."

Mrs. Rattle took my hands in hers.

"Thank you, Mable, for coming out in the dark to tell me this."

"You'll cancel the strike for tomorrow, won't you?"

She sighed and shook her head with a smile. "We have no choice. Or rather, we have made our choice. We will proceed with the strike."

"But –"

"There is too much at stake to back down now."

The moon was hidden behind clouds when I came out from Mrs. Rattle's. It was a longer journey home, not being able to see where I was stepping. Or perhaps I stumbled because I knew not where I next should travel on my life's road, if I may be permitted such a poetic allusion. I have tried this night to do good – to rescue Mrs. Rattle from harm – and have been rebuffed. Is she foolish or courageous? Have I done my best? And yet fallen short? Is there another path I have not seen that I might follow?

THURSDAY, NOVEMBER 14

May I never live through such another day as this, should I live to be seventy-seven!

I did not expect to ever fall asleep and yet awoke with Viola shaking my shoulder, telling me she'd finished breakfast, that it was nearing eight o'clock.

"Go on without me," I said as I began to dress. A plan had arrived in my mind while I slept, and I prepared now to put it in motion.

"Do not test me by coming late to school," said Viola.

I would be very late, indeed, I realized, if I managed to come at all. I sat upon the edge of the bed with a thump. Viola looked sharply my way.

"I am ill," I said. "My head is spinning."

Viola placed a palm against my forehead, as our mother always does.

"You have no fever," she said.

"No. I have a chill. And I am dizzy." I lay back, as if anticipating a faint.

Viola glanced at the bureau clock. She should have her cloak on and be ready to leave by now. I fluttered my eyelids and twitched my fingers ever so slightly.

"The men are gone already to the outer pasture," she said, "to fix that fence they spoke of. And Mrs. Goodhand, too. She is at Mrs. Campbell's for the day, making the relish. There is no one here to care for you."

"I shall sleep," I said. "I have never felt this way before. I should not go to school else I infect the little ones."

Still she would not leave! "You do not look ill," she said. "And yet it's not your way to be a malingerer."

"You'll be late," I whispered.

And finally she departed, even smoothing the hair back from my cheek before she went. I lay still, with drumming heart, until I heard the kitchen door close and then her bootsteps across the porch. I dressed and brushed and braided and buckled and laced, hurrying in case I lost my nerve. I was downstairs before ten minutes had passed. I felt swept with dread as I stood in the pantry. What would this day bring?

Don't think, I thought, and forced myself to action.

I cut a slice of bread and took an apple with me. I had decided to take Darling and the wagon. I hoped the apple would encourage her to be more patient with my clumsiness. But Alfred had taught me well, and I managed the hitch with no great difficulty. I tried to force away the notion that I was actually *stealing* Darling, having already *lied* to Viola. . . . What punishment would be assigned for the crimes I undertook?

I had never been to the Forrest house, or the factory, of course, but knew their home lay off the main road toward Stratford. I set out away from school and Sellerton with Darling trotting along as an easy accomplice. I prayed that no familiar passerby should see us.

A signpost eventually directed me to the Forrest Family and the Bright Creek Cheese Company down the same road. We came to the house first. It is perhaps twice the size of the Goodhand farm and four times Mama's.

I felt quite choked for a moment. This was my very last chance to turn back. It helped my resolve to see Cathy and Frank Forrest on the veranda, pink cheeked in the frosty morning. They waved as Darling slowed, and darted into the yard to meet us.

"Miss Mable!" They clapped their hands and pummeled me with questions.

"Why are you here? May we come to school again? Will you take us for a ride? Are you going to the factory? Are you going to see the trouble?"

I put my hand up for attention as I do in the classroom.

"What do you know about the trouble, Frank?"

"Papa wouldn't let us go with him." He pouted. "The lazy girls are getting a smacking to-day, but he won't let us watch."

My stomach turned over.

"It's not fair," said Cathy. "Usually it's us getting a smacking, and now it's someone else and we can't watch."

"It's not a nice thing to see," I told her. "I don't like it one bit watching Miss Riley strap someone, do you?"

"Better watching than getting," grumbled Frank.

"That's true," I agreed.

The door behind them opened.

"Frank and Cathy Forrest, you get back on the porch this instant!"

Mrs. Forrest stomped out, coming down the steps to shoo her children back up to the safety of the veranda. They leaned against the railing, peering over her shoulders while she faced me with her arms crossed.

"Well?" she growled.

I managed, "Good morning, Mrs. Forrest." Suddenly my plan seemed foolhardy at best.

"You're not here to wish me well, that much I know."

"I have come . . ." I hesitated and glanced at Frank's and Cathy's listening faces. Surely she would do nothing dreadful to me in front of them?

"I have come to beg you to intervene in the trouble at the factory, Mrs. Forrest. Is there not a better way to solve differences than to bully the women? Surely, as a woman yourself, you have some sympathy for their plight?"

"Their plight, missy? And how would you describe their plight?"

Oh, dear. My lips were numb. How could I form the words?

"I mean only, well, the plight of unhappiness."

That sounded foolish. She snorted.

"Is it your treasured Mrs. Rattle you're worried about?" she said. "You are smitten with her, Mable, and your admiration is misplaced. She is a rich girl playing at rough games to which she doesn't know the rules."

"What rules? What do you mean?"

"Papa has lots of rules," said Frank. His mother shushed him quickly before turning back to me.

"Mr. Forrest makes decisions that are good for business and will indirectly benefit everyone." She sounded nearly patient, as if she were speaking to a very thickheaded child. "It is not for the worker to question the master. Only someone as pampered as Mrs. Rattle would complain.

"You leave the adult business to adults, Mable. It seems to me that your interference has not been requested. Should you not be at school?"

I had no answer to that. I *should* be at school. And perhaps there were aspects to the situation that I could not understand.

But I had one more plea. I lowered my voice, so as not to frighten the children. "I am afraid the women will be hurt by the policemen. Would you be able to forgive yourself for not stepping in?"

"My conscience is certainly my own affair," said Mrs. Forrest. "No one will get hurt if they pay attention to common sense."

"But what if there *is* trouble? What if someone is maimed? Or killed?"

Oh, great goodness, what if?

But Mrs. Forrest was done with me. "Pah!" she sighed angrily. "It's whining, spoiled girls who are forcing my husband to show who's boss to-day. Sometimes a sharp word is enough and sometimes not. If he's forced to wield a strong arm, then so be it. It will all be over and back to the cheese vats tomorrow."

"Oh, Mrs. Forrest! Couldn't you just try to stop it?"

"I'm on my way over to Bright Creek right now," she said. "I'll see what's to be done. You'd be showing some sense to get yourself to school before I report you truant."

She turned away and marched up the steps, putting an arm around each child and pushing them ahead of her into the house. I knew she was trying to frighten me away, but even knowing the ruse, it worked. I shivered with fear, tears welling, and ran to the cart.

My efforts had likely come to naught. Should I hurry back to school to save my skin? Too late for that. I urged Darling into action before I had even sat myself properly down. We hurried along, the wind nipping the wet streaks on my cheeks. When we turned the next bend, I pulled on the reins and stopped us short.

Outside the Bright Creek Cheese Company was a swarm of singing women, waving painted signs in the air and wearing lettered sashes across their chests. I did not see Mrs. Rattle at once, but noticed Helen Stevens holding up a sign that shouted "FAIR WORK FOR FAIR PAY!" Her face was rosy from cold, but perhaps from excitement as well. They were certainly having a time of it, linking arms and singing out verses of "Rescue the Perishing" with great energy. I realized after several moments that there were only about a dozen women, but they were making enough disturbance for a larger crowd.

At one corner of the brick building lurked the menacing presence of six mounted policemen holding their horses at bay, presumably awaiting an order to do otherwise.

It was nearby the officers that I saw Mrs. Rattle. She was wearing her bloomers and the scarlet cloak. She was arguing (or at least it looked that way from my distance, as she gestured and grimaced) with Mr. Forrest, whose face was twisted in loathing.

I climbed down from the cart and unhitched Darling so that she could nose the ground for tidbits. As if by a magnet, I found myself drawn toward Mrs. Rattle and her former employer. Despite the lilting verses of the protestors, I came close enough to hear the altercation. I hesitated between the wall and the first horse, not willing to reveal myself as an eavesdropper.

"We're asking for a reasonable compromise," Mrs. Rattle was saying. "We could meet now, in your office, to discuss the possibilities. There is no cause to threaten us with these horsemen." She looked up at the officers, who ignored her.

"There is nothing reasonable about you," said Mr. Forrest. "You are insane. I do not intend to speak with you any further."

"There is a difference between insanity and justified anger, sir."

The women's song turned into a chant. "We want fair work! We want fair pay!" They began to sway as they called out, a few steps forward then a few steps back. Mr. Forrest called to an officer.

"This has gone far enough!" He tried to step around Mrs. Rattle, but she blocked his way.

"We want fair work! We want fair pay!" I joined the cry as I ducked back among the protestors, not wanting to be found eavesdropping by Mr. Forrest.

The horses moved toward the women at the same moment, their hooves looking heavier and closer with every step. We could be crushed, I thought. I stopped dead. This was not a story or a drama. This was real! Real harm could come of this. My jacket felt too tight and hot. My ears buzzed. One of the protestors dropped her sign, pressing herself against the wall of the factory building to avoid being trodden on.

At that moment came a shrill cry. The women's voices paused, and I looked behind me to see Mrs. Forrest hurtling toward us, holding her skirts up out of the way of her thick boots.

"What are you doing here?" shrieked Mrs. Forrest, advancing on Mrs. Rattle. "You no longer work at Bright Creek. You are trespassing on this property! If you are not departed within one minute, I will have you arrested!"

Any hope of reason evaporated as Mrs. Forrest faced her foe.

Mrs. Rattle was now flanked by the Forrests. She turned toward the marching ladies and raised her hands as if she were conducting an orchestra. They lifted their voices in a hymn as Mrs. Rattle's smile beamed out to cheer them.

But in one indignant motion, Mrs. Forrest pushed her, using both hands to send her sprawling. Mrs. Rattle's head hit the frozen ground with a sickening bump and she crumpled.

"No!" I cried. "No!" A scream of outrage rose from the factory women, but the policemen instantly formed themselves into a barricade that prevented their intrusion.

I know not what propelled me or where I found the nerve; I squeezed between two horses and there I was, clutching at Mrs. Forrest's cloak to yank her back from Mrs. Rattle. I tried to thrust her aside and raised my fists in a fury. My hands met her shoulder, and I shoved, hard, knocking her onto her bottom. Her google-eyed look of shock nearly made me laugh in the midst of the horror. She struggled in her winter layers to right herself like a flopping beetle. I turned away and knelt at once beside the still, slight figure on the ground, slipping my arms beneath her.

"Arrest her!" cried Mrs. Forrest, somewhere above me. "Arrest them all, officers!"

I stopped listening. Mrs. Rattle had not moved. I held her head in my lap, checking first that there was no blood. Her lips and cheeks had gone white, seeming especially pale next to her dark lashes and wild hair. I shut my eyes and leaned my face so close to hers that I could feel her breath. I wept with relief. She was breathing.

Now I noticed the confusion around me. The police were herding women into a row of horse-drawn wagons, which waited in the lane beyond the factory. Mr. Forrest was pacing while his wife shouted orders.

"Take that one!" Mrs. Forrest pointed a finger at me. "Take that little spitfire!"

An officer lifted Mrs. Rattle and carried her to a wagon while I trotted alongside like an anxious pup. But when he'd set her down on the wooden boards, he firmly picked me up and dropped me next to her. His thick fingers grasped my waist and flung me up with no trouble at all. Never had I been so handled by a man! Already in the cart were Helen Stevens and another woman.

"Oh, goodness!" said Helen. She pulled off her cloak and tucked it around Mrs. Rattle but started to shiver at once, having on only a factory smock over her dress. As the officer bent down to shove Mrs. Rattle's feet back from the edge, the bristles on his neck were mere inches from my face. I shuddered and drew back, but with nowhere to go.

Only then did I recognize my situation fully. Mrs. Rattle was injured. We were being taken somewhere by the police. I had changed somehow from an ordinary girl into a criminal. When the wagon began to move, I realized also that I'd abandoned Darling and the cart! First stolen, and then abandoned! However could I explain to the Goodhands?

"Excuse me, sir?" I called to the driver, but he paid no attention. Mrs. Rattle's head bounced as the wagon wheel stuttered on a rut and she cried out. I carefully lifted her head and rested it upon my thigh. I chewed my lip to hold in tears.

"Are you not the girl who served tea in Mrs. Rattle's parlour a few weeks ago?" asked Helen.

"Yes," I said. She looked every bit as cold and unhappy as I was. "Would you like to share my cloak? It's not much, but . . ." I unfastened the neck and held it open. She smiled and crawled closer so we could hunch together and try to stir up warmth.

"My horse is back there," I said, pointing. "Not mine really, which makes the matter worse. What will happen to her, do you think?"

"Someone will come upon her," Helen assured me. "She will not be harmed. It's us I'm worried about!"

Before the end of the drive, not so long as an hour, Mrs. Rattle came awake and was astonished to discover the time and so many miles gone by. She sat up and looked about. She seemed slightly groggy but waved to the women in the wagon following ours and to the mounted police-man who escorted us.

"We must sing as we disembark," she said, "to show them our spirits are not bruised, even if our skulls are." She rubbed the back of her head. "Ooh, that hurts." She had me touch her "goose egg."

"What will happen to us?" I asked. "Are we to be jailed?"

"That would be best," Mrs. Rattle said calmly. "If we are put in jail, there will have to be a notice in the newspapers."

She saw my reaction and squeezed my hand. "You have no cause to worry," she said. "I know not what brought you here this morning, Mable Riley, but this is not your battle."

"Oh, but she fought," said Helen Stevens. "When Mrs. Fatty Forrest pushed you down, Mable did the same to her!"

Mrs. Rattle looked upon me in amazement. "Did you, indeed?" she exclaimed. "I wish I had seen that!"

We all laughed and I was proud to be with them, part of a cause, one of the believers.

Mrs. Rattle began to sing as we clambered down from the wagons. All the girls joined in, and we made a motley choir as we filed into the Perth County Courthouse. But Mrs. Rattle tugged on the sleeve of one of the officers, and it was clear that she spoke of me, for he turned to stare in my direction. As the factory girls were led down a corridor, Mrs. Rattle's man took me aside.

"You'll be waiting here, miss," he said.

"But –!" I wanted to follow Mrs. Rattle, but the officer simply shook his head and pointed to a chair.

Mrs. Rattle reached out a hand to me. "Later on you will forgive me," she said quickly. "I've told them you came to Bright Creek quite by accident. You are too young to be imprisoned, Mable Riley. You'll have other chances, I am certain!" She laughed and hurried away along the hall.

My chair sat next to a large desk manned by an earnest young sergeant with a dimple in his chin.

"If you'd care to wash up a bit, miss?" he asked.

I looked down and realized my hands and clothes were splashed with mud. My face must be the same! I nodded at him and was directed to a small room off the foyer. As I emerged, I heard the voice of Mrs. Forrest and peeked out to see her, with her husband, looming over the young man at the desk.

"I will speak with the highest-ranking person on the force," she insisted. "It is a matter of the utmost urgency when leading citizens are attacked on their own property!"

The sergeant went away and came back shortly, to lead the Forrests into an office out of sight. Finally, I could return to my seat.

The wait began. I wished I were with the other women so I would at least have company. Instead, I sat dreading the reappearance of the Forrests and wondering what was to be done with me. The worst part about waiting is not knowing how long the wait will be. I fidgeted with boredom and nibbled a little on my fingernails.

When the young officer returned, he shook his head and grinned at me.

"I can't figure out if he's the boss or she is."

I smiled. He was very kind, actually. He shared tea from his jar and half his meat sandwich, for which I was very grateful, not having eaten to-day except a slice of bread. I didn't feel nearly so frightened once he was there. His name is Sergeant Sherman and he has just turned twenty, like Alfred. In the beginning he seemed a bit wary, as if I might be cracked in the head, but I explained what had happened and he said he would put in a good word for me. He said he'd never heard of such a disturbance in Perth County before, which made me worry more.

I set to waiting, not knowing for what.

I know a little of what happened elsewhere while I was sitting in that chair at the police station because Viola and Alfred have told me what occurred to them.

Viola says she worried all morning, it being so unlike me to feign illness that she imagined the symptoms indicated a sudden and serious condition. At noon she told the children they would have an extra half-hour for their lunch time and left instructions with Elizabeth to assume leadership should Viola not return. (Elizabeth claims that Viola behaved in so peculiar a fashion that the children became concerned. Irene cried all afternoon, howling that Mable was dying and poor Irene would never learn to read without her.)

Meanwhile, Viola walked home, hoping to find me recovered somewhat, but of course not finding me at all.

Now she knew not whether to be furious or terrified. Had I run off to perform some mischievous escapade? Or were my wits so deranged that I had staggered across the fields in a delusional fit? As she paced the kitchen, wringing her hands, Alfred and Mr. Goodhand arrived home for the midday meal, which Mrs. Goodhand had left for them under a tea cloth on the table.

Viola had time only to tell them that I had disappeared when Mr. Goodhand interrupted with an oath.

"What the Devil . . . ?" he said, gaping out the window. "Will you look at that?"

"That" was Darling, plodding her way up the drive.

Alfred went out to assure himself that she was unharmed and led her back to her stall. Then he realized the cart was missing and returned to the house to inform Viola.

"Why would Mable use the cart? And where is it now? Has she taken a tumble? Is she lying somewhere with a broken ankle or unconscious?"

Mr. Goodhand sat and ate his lunch while Alfred tried to console Viola. But her fancied fears took a new turn. "Oh, dear, no! Darling could not have unhitched herself from the cart. Someone must have released the horse! Mable has been abducted!"

(Alfred has since said that he dared not eat his pickles and cheese for fear of offending Viola, but his stomach began to make noises, grumbling for attention.)

Luckily, Roy arrived on his bicycle and rushed into the house with news.

"I've been at the Watson store in Sellerton," he said, still breathing heavily from his ride. "Mrs. Watson has had a call on her shop telephone from Mrs. Rattle. Your Mable is with her at the courthouse in Stratford!"

Here, Viola says she gasped. (Alfred says it was more of a scream.)

"There was a big to-do over at Bright Creek," Roy explained. "The women were striking and had a bit of a struggle with the Forrests. The police were on the scene —"

"What of Mable?" cried Viola. "Is Mable all right?"

Roy paused. He had not realized the level of Viola's distress.

"I believe she's under arrest with the rest of the ladies," he said. "She's not hurt that I know of. Mrs. Rattle's the one that got hit on the head. . . ."

But Viola had run out the door and was halfway to the barn before she remembered there was no cart to take her to Stratford.

"Roy!" She hurried back inside. "May I borrow your bicycle?"

"Have you ever ridden a bicycle?"

"No, but I –"

"It would take more than two hours to cycle all the way to town," he said. "And that's if you know how. The bicycle is not the answer here."

At this point, Viola confesses that she collapsed at the table with her head in her hands and began to sob.

The three men looked at one another over her head and had a swift and silent conference. Mr. Goodhand set out across the field to borrow Baron and the Campbells' buggy and to tell his wife the news. Roy conceived of a plan to cycle to Bright Creek, leading Darling by the reins. When they reached the factory, he would put the bicycle in the cart and have Darling drive him home again. Alfred allowed Viola to cry until she was empty, while he collected an extra blanket and lantern for the ride, guessing the return journey would be in darkness.

All this time and longer, I sat on the hard chair next to Sergeant Sherman's desk, replaying the morning's events and wondering what was to become of me. But (and I admit this with an overcoat of shame) only slowly did I expand my wondering as to how my actions may have affected anyone else. I thought of Viola, but only that she would be annoyed with me for missing school. I thought of the Goodhands, but only to anticipate their irritation with the missing cart. I thought of Mama, and how I could likely never bear to tell the truth of this day's folly.

But was it indeed folly?

I knew the answer at once. No.

Folly is "foolish" and folly is "thoughtless," but what I did to-day was neither of those things. (Perhaps it was folly that I pushed Mrs. Forrest, but that was not my purpose in going.) I woke up knowing I should go to Bright Creek today, following Mrs. Rattle's belief that girls and women need to be heard. I like to imagine there are little groups of women in villages and factories and cities and farms all over the country who began by whispering at Reading Circles and slowly are raising their voices until they are singing like rain and hollering like thunder.

I would do it again.

As I declared this to myself, Alfred and my sister came into the foyer, blinking while their eyes adjusted to the dim light so that they did not spy me until I flung myself at Viola.

"Mable! Oh! Mable!" Viola hugged me hard, laughing and crying together.

"You've come!" I cried. "Thank you! How did you know where to find me? Oh, thank you! Viola! Alfred! Both of you!"

Viola and I clutched each other, and Alfred stood by, timidly patting a shoulder on each of us.

"Let's take you home," he said. "My parents will be relieved to see you."

"Oh, Alfred, the cart!" I confessed. "It was left at Bright Creek."

"Roy has gone to fetch it," said Viola. "We'll tell you everything on the way. You have much to tell us also, I am certain." A note of reprimand crept into her voice.

"May I take her?" Alfred asked Sergeant Sherman. "Is there a paper I need to sign?"

"Oh," he said. "I don't know. She hasn't been charged with a crime that I know of, else they'd have her in with the others. I'd best check with the lieutenant." He clicked his boot heels together and scurried off. He was back in under a minute, but here my heart sank into the mire. He was followed by a stout man in uniform, as well as by the Forrests! The lieutenant's rank had not intimidated Mrs. Forrest, for she was scolding him, as strident as a jaybird.

"We want some assurance that justice will be swift, that these women will be punished —" She stopped and stared at me, causing Mr. Forrest to stumble against her.

"Here is the very person who assaulted me! This child is dangerous! Why is she not locked away in a cell?"

Sergeant Sherman looked from me to Mrs. Forrest and back again, as did the lieutenant.

"Good afternoon, Mrs. Forrest," said Viola, ever the one for manners.

"Do not speak to me, Miss Riley. Your sister attacked me this morning."

"But you pushed Mrs. Rattle first!" I protested. "How can you say I —"

"Do you hear how saucy she is, lieutenant? She has a devil in her bosom!"

"You say yourself that Mable is a child, Mrs. Forrest," said Viola, speaking up for me! "Surely, if her temper —"

"You were not there, Miss Riley. You did not see her transformation into a rabid barn cat. As you are not a witness, you are not included in this conversation."

"I am a witness," said Mr. Forrest.

We all looked at him. He licked his lips and hunched his shoulders up and down. He did not look at Mrs. Forrest.

"The girl pushed my wife," he said.

Mrs. Forrest turned in triumph to the lieutenant. "There," she said. "You see?"

"But," said Mr. Forrest, raising his voice just a little, "my wife pushed the other woman first. Pretty hard, I reckon, because her head just clunked."

Mrs. Forrest tried to interrupt with an objection, but her husband kept on talking. "I've been hearing it over and over all morning, that clunk. I've been thinking, How could it come to this? I'm a hard-working man. I expect the people I employ to be hard working as well. But I never expected my wife to go about shoving anyone to the ground, causing an injury."

"Francis Forrest!" said his wife.

He put up a hand to silence her. "You hush now," he said. "I don't know how we'll deal with all those others in the lockups back there, but I won't be pressing charges against a little girl."

"But, Francis —"

"I'm the man in this family and I make the decisions," he said. "You can let her go, lieutenant. If I were her father, she'd feel the leather tonight for messing about where she'd no business to be." He sent a meaningful look at Viola. "But I won't send her to jail."

Relieved as I was, I could not help but have some slight discomfort at being saved by the very man who had caused us all to be here.

"I guess we won't be hauling any of your milk this evening, Goodhand," he continued, to Alfred. "What we took over last night has gone to waste. Same goes for the McCoys and the Deegans."

Alfred had been standing quietly beside Sergeant Sherman. As we heard Mr. Forrest's announcement, I saw him wince, but as though he knew it was coming.

"So much milk," he said.

"Can't use it. Won't buy it," said Mr. Forrest abruptly. "This kind of trouble runs deep. You see that, little lady?" He was addressing me. "Your lunatic associates have put your generous hosts out of business. Now whose side are you on?"

I leaned against Viola, not wanting to think, but dizzy with thoughts nonetheless. Would I have to choose a side? What if the Goodhands pitched us out because I'd lost Darling? Their horse, their cart, and now their biggest milk customer. And they'd done nothing wrong! But Mrs. Rattle had not intended to do wrong, either. She was struggling to do right, for everyone. For all the women in the country!

"You just think about it," said Mr. Forrest. He took his spluttering wife away.

The lieutenant asked Viola to leave our names and address with Sergeant Sherman.

Misses Viola and Mable Riley, she wrote. *Goodhand Farm.*

"We've become a burden to your family, Alfred," she sighed. "Did you imagine when you met us at the train station in August that you would be collecting Mable from police custody only a few months later?"

Alfred chuckled. "I'm grateful for the excitement," he said.

Then he winked at her and in that wink flashed a thousand lights. I knew at once what I had not known a moment before. Alfred had not moved except for the flicker of an eyelid, but that wink might have been the crashing of cymbals or the slamming of a heavy door, so suddenly did it wake me from my slumber of ignorance. Alfred was in love with my sister!

I quickly turned to see her and, yes! She loves him back! It was written upon her features as clear as these words upon the page. I had not known her face could look so soft, her eyes so filled with stars, yet here she was.

The revelation took but an instant – not a hundredth of the time it takes to report – and only I was any wiser, for they paid no heed to me or to my discovery as Viola completed the address in her schoolmarm script.

Alfred shook the sergeant's hand and led me out to the street.

I was grateful to Baron for his rhythmic trot going home. Despite the hurly-burly within my mind, the rocking of the buggy lulled me off to sleep and let me finally rest. My last thought was that Viola loves Alfred.

FRIDAY, NOVEMBER 15

Sure enough, no milk was hauled to Bright Creek last evening or this. Alfred missed supper to do all the milking himself because Mr. Goodhand refused to do it.

"I didn't raise twenty cows to pour their milk into the ground," he said.

Mr. Goodhand will not speak to me. Indeed, it was through Viola that I was told of my punishment. I am to spend each evening making butter until my arms drop off. (It is not the churning that I object to or the straining. It is the endless *washing* of butter in great quantity that is so wearisome.) I must make no hint of complaint, says Viola, as Mrs. Goodhand and Mrs. Campbell will be churning as well.

I went to school to-day, of course. I was greeted by a crowd of curious scholars. Tommy flung an arm about my shoulder in his relief to see me, and the others were most intrigued to hear of yesterday's adventures. I have learned, however, to hold my tongue concerning matters of importance. Viola canceled the spelling bee and made us write an essay instead, on the topic of "Do unto Others As You Would Have Them Do unto You."

Tommy walked most of the way home with Elizabeth and me. Elizabeth pretended not to notice, but Tommy's left arm was only a hair's breadth from my right, all the way until the Deegan turnoff. The backs of our hands were often touching, though we did not look at each other. He has a most engaging smile, and his eyes, behind those spectacles, are a beguiling dark blue. I am very fond of this boy – it's as plain as that.

Alfred would have driven to the Groveland Cheese House to-day, but after much discussion with his father, has decided to wait until Monday. They hope not to be forced into seeking new customers; they hope there will be a swift ending to the story at Bright Creek. (Is there ever an ending to any story? I wonder. Except for birth and death, of course, the beginning or ending of a tale depends only upon where the teller decides to make it.)

I laid the table for supper while Mrs. Goodhand (over)boiled the cabbage and (scorch) fried the sausages. Mr. Goodhand was in his chair beside the stove earlier than usual, because of leaving Alfred to the milking. I thought to seize the opportunity that my mother would urge me to take.

"Mr. Goodhand? Mrs. Goodhand? I would like . . ." Mr. Goodhand rustled the newspaper, while his wife stared glumly toward my knees.

I cleared the nerves from my throat and began again.

"I realize that I have caused trouble far beyond your deserving, and I wish to apologize with all my heart and soul."

"Eh?" said Mr. Goodhand.

"Your horse and wagon, your good name, and now your farm profits, all ruined because of me!"

"Is there something wrong with Darling that I don't know about?" barked Mr. Goodhand.

"Why, no, Sir, except that I left her –"

"Then I'd say you're getting a bit big for your britches, young lady. None of this factory mess has anything to do with you. Francis Forrest was a nasty brute before you came along, and I'll wager your Mrs. Rattle was, too. You may like to think you're right in there, in the heart of the matter, but the fact is you're a little girl no one pays mind to. Your only crime is outspokenness where it's not asked for. So you needn't spout whimsy about your heart and soul because poetry won't make anybody pay to make cheese out of my milk. When you've solved that problem, you let me know." He folded the newspaper.

"Is supper ready yet, missus?" he asked his wife.

"Nearly on," she said, still not looking at me.

During the meal I felt as though I'd been spanked. But the more I considered, the better I realized it was true. The Forrests and the ladies would have butted heads whether I'd been there or gone back to school. The battle had been fought, but the real problem had not yet been solved. And Mable Riley had yet to make her mark. I did not like to admit how little my part had mattered in the outcome.

This also meant that I was no more responsible for the surplus milk than Viola was. It did not seem wise, however, to point out that my penalty of making heroic measures of butter was too high a price to pay for truancy.

After washing up, I sat on a stool next to Mr. Goodhand with my knees wrapped around the extra churn (borrowed from Roy's mother), rolling the handle back and forth while we listened to the news of the day.

"BAD NEWS AT BRIGHT CREEK
This week's trouble at the Bright Creek Cheese Company near Sellerton escalated yesterday with a violent incident and police intervention. Dissatisfied labourers have been marching outside

in protest since Tuesday instead of manning the cheese vats within.

"Is that supposed to be funny?" asked Mr. Goodhand. "'Manning' the cheese vats? Every one of them is a girl."

"After two days of halted cheese production, factory owner Mr. Francis Forrest called for uniformed assistance.

'However I tried, the workers would not listen to reason,' reported Mr. Forrest from the Perth County Courthouse last evening. 'I tried to discover an equitable solution, but my efforts were ignored by the ringleader, Mrs. Cora Rattle.'"

"That's not true!" I cried. "He refused to speak with her!"

"Mrs. Rattle and eleven other women were rounded up by the police after a confrontation between the sharp-tongued suffragist and the factory owner's wife. Mrs. Forrest was assaulted in the course of the argument, leading officers to make their move.

Mrs. Rattle and her cohorts are being held a

**second night in the county jail and will be released
tomorrow with warnings from Judge Hinks. They
are to return to work on Monday or lose their
positions. The factory will recommence production then.”**

"Aha!" shouted Alfred. "I saved a trip to Groveland to-
day, and Sunday's milk will still be good on Monday, with
this chill. We're set, Dad. It'll all work out."

**"Mrs. Rattle's employ was terminated three weeks
ago before the disturbance began. She will not
return to Bright Creek.”**

"What do you suppose Mrs. Rattle will do now?" I
wondered.

"She'll go and stir up trouble elsewhere," said Mr.
Goodhand.

"You think she'll move away?" I asked wistfully, knowing the answer already.

"She will not be welcome in this community," said Mrs.
Goodhand. "Not that she was welcome before, but some of
us tried."

I thought with a twinge of guilt of her corn bread and
of Mrs. Rattle's fat and happy ducks. . . .

"Oh!" I cried. "Mrs. Rattle's ducks! No one will have fed them!"

"I don't see as how feeding her ducks is any of our business," complained Mrs. Goodhand. Little knowing, I thought, that she did so every week.

I implored her to allow me to take the end of yesterday's loaf, "as a particular treat." I hurried across the fields to Silver Lining, my heart lifting just to see it, even though Mrs. Rattle would not be there. I tore the bread and rolled it between my thumbs into tiny pellets before tossing it to the hungry ducks. I wanted to prolong my stay through the night until morning, when she should return. I'll have to get used to her not being here, I realized. I'll have to think new things all on my own.

It was on the journey home that I conceived my notion.

The more I thought on it, the more possible it seemed. I found Alfred back in the barn, his face morose while he cleaned the hooves of a cow named Poppy.

"I have an idea," I said.

"Mmmm?" said Alfred.

"Do you suppose the other farmers feel as your father does about Bright Creek?"

"They'll be relieved to sell the milk again, if that's what you mean."

"No, I mean his displeasure when he discovered that

Mr. Forrest mistreats his workers, that they work such long hours."

Alfred laughed. "Everyone works long hours, Mable. Farmers longest of all. But you're right that my father thinks Mr. Forrest should pay more when the labour is so tedious and tiring. And not bully the ladies while they work."

"Well, tell me what you think of this. Now that Mr. Forrest is ready to buy milk again, what if the farmers said that they would sell only if conditions at Bright Creek improve?"

Alfred's hands stopped moving.

"Farmers do not want to play games, Mable. They need to sell their milk."

"But they need to sell their milk forever. Suppose no changes are made and business returns to the way it was before? Suppose a month from now the factory ladies protest again? And the farmers are once more saddled with gallons of sour milk."

Alfred looked at me with one eyebrow lifted. "Is that being planned? Has Mrs. Rattle suggested such a thing?"

"She is still imprisoned. I have not spoken with her. But if I were organizing a campaign for workers' rights, that's the way I'd plan it," I said. "Think about it, Alfred. Do the farmers not wield the most power in this equation? If Bright Creek cannot buy milk, they will go out of business. But the farmers can sell elsewhere – to Groveland or the place in Perth Valley, though it is many miles farther, I realize. But, on the face of things, is it not Bright Creek who must compromise to keep what they depend upon?"

I held my breath. Would he agree?

Alfred was quiet while he finished with Poppy. Then he stood and patted her flank.

"You've a devious mind, Mable," he said. "If ever you have a suitor, I'll be sure to warn him. But on this matter . . . Let me speak with my father. He won't like the pressure, but he may see the sense in it."

"Suppose you go to Mr. Forrest yourself," I said. "Suppose you speak on the farmers' behalf?"

"I will need to first speak to the farmers. Peter Deegan and Brice McCoy may not be willing to risk so much."

"But will you, Alfred?"

"Let me think, Mable."

Ambler's Corners
November 13, 1901

My dear Mable,

I am troubled by the quarrelsome tone of your most recent letter. You seem almost eager to declare yourself at odds with me (and, indeed, with everyone else!).

You say that "to risk censure and discomfort by following one's heart is better by far than to obey expectations without a heartbeat." With such dismay did I read those words!

Do you not understand that honest women like your Mrs. Goodhand or Mrs. Forrest are so respected *because they are respectable??* Surely it is better to stand safely amid the flock in a sunny meadow than to willfully follow the black sheep through a thistle patch? Without knowing what inclement weather awaits you?

I am heavy-hearted with the fear that I am in some way responsible for your behaviour. By encouraging your story writing, I hoped to harness your fancies to a manageable task. It seems, however, that a nature wilder than I realized has been unbridled.

I beg you to seek guidance in your evening prayers. Turn away from the dangerous temptation of imagination. Remember, it is wiser to be dull than overly merry!

Most sincerely, with concern,

    Your friend,

    Hattie

If only Hattie knew how late her warnings come! And how little I would heed them in any case. She begins to sound more like Reverend Scott with every note. Her talk of flocks and thistles might win her a position as sermon writer for a dullard minister. How lucky am I to be the lamb who sprouted wings to fly!

SATURDAY, NOVEMBER 16

The Bright Creek ladies were released this morning. Alfred saw them in town, leaving the courthouse, all together. He says they looked disheveled but were laughing, walking with linked arms. He did not notice Mrs. Rattle in particular. And though his errand would affect them mightily, he did not think to stop and speak.

Alfred collected the post at the office and then drove to the Deegan dairy farm, where he had arranged to meet the other farmers concerned by the Bright Creek situation.

"Pete Deegan got the sense of it at once," Alfred reported at the lunch table. "But Mr. McCoy and his son, Bart? They must have said fifty times that it was crazy."

"It *is* crazy," grumbled Mr. Goodhand. "But it's worth a try, just to have the upper hand with Francis Forrest for an hour or two."

"That was the winning point," agreed Alfred. "Nobody likes the man. No one wants to see him gloating."

"Well, then, son," said Mr. Goodhand, "I'll go over there with you this afternoon. There's strength in numbers. Best have it done quickly."

"That's right, Dad. The milk gets collected Sunday

evening. The girls are expected back to work on Monday morning, so things should be sorted out now. Pete Deegan will come too. I think we hold the winning ticket."

I decided it was best to follow the womanly example set by Mrs. Goodhand and Viola. I did not offer an opinion on the matter under discussion. But Alfred winked at me as he shuffled out the door with his father.

LATER

It is nearly *unbearable* to wait for word from Alfred and his father.

I have penned another chapter for Hattie, mostly to avoid writing her a letter containing a brisk lecture on small-mindedness.

PART THE ELEVENTH
{MYRTLE'S REDEMPTION}

Unbeknownst to Helena, the bandits' hideout was only twelve miles from her home. Their thundering ride following the holdup had retraced the miles covered by her train ride the night before.

Helena's father, the earl, had recovered slightly from the heart attack occasioned by the news of

Helena's elopement, but hovered now within Death's desiring grasp. The Lady Myrtle, upon causing her father to collapse, had undergone a transformation.

So intense was her remorse that she had vowed to nurse him day and night until he once more looked at her with recognition. She rested only briefly in the armchair beside the earl's bed, praying each time she woke that he might have recovered his wits so that she could make amends.

But there he lay, his skin ashen, his eyelids fluttering occasionally, and his every breath a rasping labour.

When Myrtle notified the police that her sister was missing, possibly a passenger on the train that had been robbed, they had tracked Helena's flight as far as the scoundrel, James, and there the trail went cold. Unwilling to confess his own cowardly behaviour in the face of the outlaws, James had lied and told the investigators that Helena had never boarded the train with him.

As distraught as Myrtle was over her father's illness, she was nearly deranged by Helena's disappearance. Every hour she tripped across some new reason to cry. Elizabeth, the maid, brought chilled cucumber slices to soothe Myrtle's swollen eyes and urged her to partake of soup or biscuits, but was turned away at each attempt.

She who had resented every smile bestowed upon her sister now yearned to see her comely face once more.

"If my father is delivered from his illness," Myrtle whispered to the moon, "and my sister retrieved from whatever misery has befallen her, I pledge to perform charitable deeds for as long as I shall breathe upon this earth."

With this solemn vow forsworn, the Lady Myrtle allowed herself to eat her supper and to sink into sleep, not really expecting that tomorrow would bring an answer, of sorts, to her dreams.

To be continued . . .

LATER STILL . . .

The farmers have triumphed!

The men returned for supper in a fever of merriment. I believe Mr. Goodhand thinks he has played out a school-yard fight with Mr. Forrest and finally succeeded in punching him in the nose. (No such thing occurred, in fact, however much it was deserved.)

The afternoon in the Bright Creek office was spent shouting, stamping feet, and thumping on the table until finally they all sat down like gentlemen to agree upon the details. . . .

The ladies will work one hour less per day and have a full half-hour dinner recess.

They will change tasks every two hours and have five minutes' rest between each change.

Anyone in contact with scalding water or harsh cleansers will be provided with gloves or other protective clothing.

They may be fined only for tardiness of ten minutes or more.

They may speak to each other while they work.

Such a list of improvements! In exchange, the ladies will not protest again and the farmers will sell their milk at the same price as before.

Alfred says Mr. Forrest was grudging in the end but not objectionable. I suspect the ladies will be jubilant.

Mr. Goodhand had quiet words for me, while the others were tidying. "It seems odd to you, Mable, that Mr. Forrest would not consider speaking to the women who were causing the trouble. Mr. Forrest is the sort who thinks it takes men to speak to men. And he would spit beetles before he'd speak to the little girl who had the bright idea how to fix things. I didn't expect to be thanking you, but the idea worked, and here I am." It was as kind a gesture as he has ever made.

Meanwhile, as closely as I watched Alfred and Viola last night and this evening, I have gained no further indication of their love. I wondered briefly if I imagined my discovery but have decided otherwise. The very lack of evidence has confirmed my suspicion. They are careful in company not to even look at each other.

And so. "Viola," I said as we readied for bed. "What do you suppose will happen next?"

"Whatever do you mean?"

"If we were living in a story, what would be the next chapter? We have left home, traveled afar, met interesting strangers, been challenged by adversity, and encountered the police. Should there not be a love scene?"

"Are you suggesting that your shameless flirting with Tommy Thomas and the Brown twins be counted as love? You are only fourteen, Mable. I think you'll have to wait for your love scene."

"What about you?" I asked. "Could the love scene be yours?"

She became still as a chair. She knew that I had learned her secret.

"Mable," she said, looking into my eyes. "If ever you needed to be trustworthy, this is the moment. Sit down."

I sat. "You can trust me."

She took my hand. "I do not know how you . . . But Alfred and I –" She broke off, blushing deep pink.

"I know," I said. "When you came to fetch me at the courthouse, I saw it then. But why must it be such a great secret? Do you not wish to shout the news from the spire of Sellerton Methodist?"

"Mable, you have such childish notions still. We could not continue living in this house if anyone knew. It would be unthinkable! And we have not yet made plans for the future. I must consider Mama. She needs the money I earn. I cannot risk her losing that."

"But surely the school board cannot fire you for falling in love? That is too cruel!"

Viola smiled as if I were very dull witted. "Not for falling in love, Mable. I will be fired when we marry. There is a law against married women being teachers."

"You're getting married?" I knew not which bite to take first. "There's a law against it?"

"Of course we'll marry someday. We simply don't know when. We must think of Mama."

"There shouldn't be such a law! There's no law preventing married men from teaching!"

"That's true," she said. "Men don't have babies. Marriage does not change their ability to teach."

"It seems likely to me that a woman with children in her home would understand better than anyone how to teach them," I said, believing it with all my heart as suddenly as I had thought it up. "There should be a law that *only* parents can be teachers, especially mothers."

"Silly Mable." And she hugged me!

LOVE POEM
As from Viola to Alfred

Perhaps my temper is too tart,
Perhaps my sister lost your cart,
Perhaps, at times, I am too smart:
You simply wink and smile.

Perhaps Cupid shot a dart,
Perhaps my gravy won your heart,
Perhaps, nay, surely, we won't part:
You'll have my love awhile.

SUNDAY, NOVEMBER 17
I hoped to avoid the Forrests after church this morning (sermon: "Let Honesty Lead You to Heaven"), but Mrs. Forrest was waiting at the churchyard gate to pounce on us while her husband fetched the carriage.

Alfred escorted his mother right past her with only a curt nod. Viola held my hand and we intended to stroll past, but she stopped us with a greeting.

"You there."

"Good morning," said Viola.

"I suppose you think you're pretty clever." Mrs. Forrest spoke to me.

I wondered briefly if she referred to what was foremost in my mind, but answered as though she did.

"I was only trying to help."

"Well," she said, "you might have."

I looked at Viola, confused. Mrs. Forrest seemed to be saying . . .

"You heard me correctly," she said. "Your fiddling may have resulted in some good this time. If those hard-headed girls actually perform their duties – and they will have no excuse for complaints with the new hours – Mr. Forrest will be satisfied."

"How did you know it was my idea?"

"It had to be a female mind that came up with a sneaky plan like this one," said Mrs. Forrest. "Alfred is a good boy, but he's as thick as an elm tree."

Viola tightened her grip on my hand and Mrs. Forrest saw.

"Oh, ho!" she pounced. "That's the way it is, eh?"

Viola and I both shook our heads in protest. Mrs. Forrest seemed to swell with excitement before our very eyes.

"I knew it! You set your cap for that boy the moment you arrived in Sellerton!"

"No," said Viola.

"I predicted this the night I heard you two singing in the lane like a couple of spooning cats."

"You're mistaken," said Viola.

"We'll see about that," said Mrs. Forrest. "We'll see whether your sister's cleverness can wheedle you out of this one. We'll see how you slide out of the scandal of living under the same roof as your secret paramour! We'll just see . . . !"

She was positively gleeful as Mr. Forrest arrived in the carriage. He climbed down to help his wife climb up, and he tipped his hat to me. Not knowing, I thought with numbing dread, the earful he'd be receiving on the road home.

I stared at Viola aghast, but she was strangely calm.

"We must tell the Goodhands directly when we get home from church," she said. "There will be no scandal if we have already made arrangements to live elsewhere."

"Where will we live?"

"Someone will have a room for us. I will not be defeated by that haranguing old bat. We'll tell the truth quickly before Mrs. Forrest can circulate her version. 'Let Honesty

Lead You to Heaven.' I love Alfred Goodhand, and so to Heaven I go."

Ambler's Corners
November 20, 1901

My darling girls,

Never was I more surprised than reading your news, Viola. If Flossie had shaken the feather duster in my direction, I might have fallen over!

I am happy for you, dear child, perhaps more so because I am certain that love came as a surprise to you too. And I am curious beyond words to meet Mr. Alfred Goodhand, to know for myself what you have both told me – that he is worthy of you. I think your idea of bringing him here for Christmas is a splendid one. If he can survive a visit in the wild Riley house, he is a fine man, indeed.

All the children send hugs and kisses and shouts and cheers!

Affectionately,

Your mama

FRIDAY, NOVEMBER 22

I do not think my pencil can race so quickly as my thoughts – or my beating heart – for Viola is not the only one to have a romance! There, I have said it. Though perhaps I run too far ahead to call it "romance." The plain truth is I have had a kiss! *Yes! A kiss!* I was beginning to despair that it should ever happen and now it has! Shall I tell all? Of course! Never again will I have a first kiss to describe and linger over.

The tale begins when the spelling bee ended. Viola had announced that this would be the deciding match. The Commas were in a frenzy of delight (hurrah!), having won by two points. Elizabeth departed in a fit of pique – not that I blame her as I would have felt *identically* had the tables been turned – but I was left with no companion.

"Despite your win," said Viola, "you still must do the sweeping and wash the blackboard."

I watched with envy the other scholars leave the yard – Tommy and Joseph taunting Henry for being on the losing team and the younger girls skipping off home with rosy noses. I did my tasks, wondering how to cheer up Elizabeth (and came upon the plan of a friendship letter, horribly misspelled, to win her smile back).

Viola bade me leave without her as she prefers to grade papers at school while there is still light rather than at the farm by candle.

And so! And so! I set out alone and had come nearly home when who should jump out at me from behind a tree but Tommy! I wish I could say I did not scream, but scream I did, heart bumping in fright.

He laughed, coming close and taking off his spectacles.

"What is it?" I asked, thinking his manner odd.

"Mable," he said, "I've been thinking about something."

"Well? What is it?" I asked again.

"Please don't be angry," he said.

And then, without another moment spent, he leaned toward me and put his lips against my mouth. They were cold, but softer than expected, and tasted faintly of pecans, as if he had been cracking and chewing nuts while he waited for me.

I closed my eyes and then opened them, not knowing which was better. But his eyes were open too, lash to lash with mine. It was so surprising that we stopped the kiss and stared. Who blushed more? I wonder. We could not help but laugh.

And that was it. My first kiss. Now that I think upon it, I wish we had kissed again. I wish I had kept my eyes shut and felt the field tilt beneath my feet. But perhaps it was a good thing, to have shared it with a fellow who could laugh along with me. I do feel a shiver of . . . of triumph! I've had my first kiss and will remember it for all of my life!

"Very cheeky, Tommy Thomas," I said. "Do you make a habit of scaring the wits out of a girl and then kissing her?"

He put his spectacles back on and kicked a stone. "It was all right, though, wasn't it?" He looked at me sideways.

I did not mean to giggle, but it slipped out. "Yes."

Tommy walked with me to the gate. I wonder now when we might kiss again? Certainly not within sight of Mrs. Goodhand's kitchen window! It's a relief there is no school tomorrow, as I must recover from this historic occasion.

SATURDAY, NOVEMBER 23

I have not told Viola about Tommy and do not think I will. I most certainly will not tell Hattie! (She used to ask, "Would the setting of a kiss be more important or the person?" Well, clearly the person matters more! One is not kissing the scenery!) Hattie is too much of a fussbudget these days to hear my confidence. Perhaps Elizabeth, if the time is ever right. Has she been kissed? I wonder.

Viola and Alfred have decided to have a photograph taken to mark their engagement. There is a fellow in Stratford who has reasonable rates, Alfred says. They will have it done next week and printed in time to send to Mama, that she might have a preview of Alfred before Christmas!

SUNDAY, NOVEMBER 24

The Reverend Mr. Scott caught my attention this morning during his sermon entitled "To Keep One's Promise Is to Praise the Lord."

". . . It is grave news for good people that since the law first permitted *divorce*, in 1867, there have been fifty-three couples in Canada to suffer its mortification! Fifty-three couples in only thirty-four years have succumbed to failure, nay, have *sought* failure, rather than hold fast to the vows made before God. Where can this lead us except into darkness? . . ."

I suddenly wondered, Was Mrs. Rattle possibly *not* a widow? Had she been *divorced* instead? Was she even so audacious as that?

I told myself I would find out the truth to-day. To-day or never, I realized.

As I walked to Silver Lining, snow began to fall, sprinkling all the world with confectioner's sugar.

Mrs. Rattle has begun to dismantle her home. The wicker chairs were lined up, pushed against the wall, and covered with sheets. The books were stacked in crates. The tasseled drapes were taken down, allowing the winter light to pour across the naked dancer on the wall.

"What do you suppose the next tenant will make of her?" asked Mrs. Rattle.

"Is there to be a next tenant already?" It was a dreadful thought.

"Not yet," said Mrs. Rattle. "I paid the year in advance and there are still a few months on the lease. But I must travel on from here or die of being an outcast." She clapped her hands suddenly. "I will not indulge in feeling sorry for myself. There is too much packing up to do! I had thought to leave Underwood with you, Mable, but now have had word that the *Berlin Dispatch* has accepted my application and I will work as a journalist again. Is this not good news?"

"It is," I said. "Except that you are leaving and I shall possibly never see you again."

"I do not believe that to be true," she said, so quickly that she gave me hope. "The likes of us are quite sure to meet again. Berlin is not *so* far away. It is not Germany, after all. You will be looking for work yourself in only a few years. Who better to approach than an old hand like me? Why, by then, I might own the newspaper!"

"I wish you were not so cheerful!" I burst out.

"Oh, dear. I'm sorry." She was subdued at once. "I have spent my night hours crying and now seize the daylight to give me courage to go on."

"May I ask you a question, Mrs. Rattle? Though my sister would scold me for impertinence?"

"Now I'm curious." She grinned.

"What happened to Mr. Rattle?"

"Ahh. Is it wise for me to tell you? Will you keep my secret?"

I nodded eagerly.

"There never was a Mr. Rattle," she said. "Cora Rattle is the name I was born with, and I plan to take it to my grave. But by adding the 'Mrs.' up front, I add opportunity. A widow can live by herself without suspicion. Why should I avoid such a pleasure because of a silly title?"

"Isn't it odd," I said, "how Viola is waiting to be married for her life to begin while you think of marriage as an ending?"

"Not an ending for everyone, dear girl, but certainly not one of my dreams. I think your sister will be lucky in her choice of Alfred Goodhand."

"He's very kind," I agreed. I looked around the room at clear surfaces and bare walls. "It seems so . . . so empty," I said. I bit my lip to hold the tears inside.

"Dear Mable Riley," said Mrs. Rattle, grasping my shoulders, "when I was your age, I knew nothing beyond lessons in French and drawing with my governess. I was filled to the brim with other people's knowledge. I would have made a good parrot, but my head was as empty as this room.

"This is why I find you so admirable, Mable. You are already asking questions and seeking answers. I wish you had been my friend when I was fourteen so that I had not wasted years having a lazy mind."

"We're friends now," I ventured.

"Yes," she said. "We're friends."

"I suppose one good thing is that we are writers," I said. "We could write letters to each other, could we not?"

"Of course!" she cried. "Writers never have to say goodbye. We simply write another letter." She stepped forward and hugged me tight, a quick and impetuous embrace that knocked the breath right out of me.

Whatever brave face I held while in her presence, it vanished upon departure. I cried without stopping all the way to my bed.

"PERSONAL AND SOCIAL NOTES

"Will you listen to this," said Mr. Goodhand. "Listen, son. Viola, dear? Are you listening?

"Mr. Alfred Goodhand has announced his betrothal to Miss Viola Riley. Miss Riley will retire as the Sellerton schoolteacher at the end of this school year. A replacement is being sought. Mr.

A. Goodhand will continue to work on the farm of his father, Mr. H. Goodhand.

The happy couple will be wed in July and will lease the cottage known as Silver Lining to begin their married life. Miss Riley and her sister, Miss Mable Riley, will live in the cottage until the wedding, with an eye to making certain improvements for the newlyweds."

"Oh, clip that one out, Howard," said Mrs. Goodhand. "I'll put it in the scrapbook."

"Mrs. Cora Rattle has departed the area for Berlin, Ontario, where she will be employed as a reporter for the *Berlin Dispatch*. Her friends will miss her and wish her well.

"May the evildoers of Berlin *beware!*" cried Mr. Goodhand. "The Avenging Angel is upon thee!" He chuckled at his own wit. Alfred patted my hand.

WEDNESDAY, NOVEMBER 27

Tomorrow is Thanksgiving Day.

Viola is insisting, in a friendly, daughterly fashion, that Mrs. Goodhand is still in mourning and should be spared the effort of cooking so much this year. Viola and I will create the feast to celebrate our new relations. Elizabeth will come and chop things up with us. She is very nearly a cousin now. I am to be the pie maker and Viola will do the rest. She is anxious that it all be just right. Alfred is delighted. He will grow quite fat when Viola becomes Mrs. Goodhand if he does not take care!

We have been to Mrs. Rattle's cottage, to finalize our arrangements. Sadly, the first "improvement" we must make will be to paint over the naked dancer on the wall. Viola blushed crimson when she saw it and thanked Heaven Mr. Goodhand did not accompany us!

It is fitting that I have reached the final pages of this record book. I will begin a new one with the heading of Silver Lining! When I began this account, I knew not what the story would be or whom I would meet. It is a sentimental notion, but every day is a new page, sometimes a whole chapter. I have realized that I will be the writer of my own story as much as the reader of others'.

The romantic tale I have been writing for Hattie seems sillier and sillier. And yet I must end it for her, must I not?

PART THE TWELFTH
{ALL'S WELL THAT ENDS WELL}

Helena waited in the yard while the soldiers went inside to raid the bandits' hideaway. She peered into the gathering gloom of dusk for signs of the departing Captain Brigand and his band of brothers. It was a relief and yet a sorrow that she could see nothing.

Within minutes, the lieutenant again stood before her, all pretense of politeness gone as he roughly shook her arm.

"Those villains were here!" he snarled. "The coffee is still hot in the cups! Where have they gone?"

The other soldiers surrounded her now.

"And who are you?" asked a curious young sergeant with a dimple in his chin.

"I am Helena duBarry," she calmly replied, ignoring the first question.

"What?" The lieutenant's face turned a shade darker. "Daughter of Fitzgerald duBarry, earl of Abercorn?"

"The same," answered Helena, confused by his knowledge.

"We have been hunting you these past three days!" cried the man. "Your father wishes to see you before he dies!"

Helena duBarry was brought home to the earl's mansion by Lieutenant McCarthy only sixty-seven hours after she had departed it, but she felt as though six years had gone by.

The Lady Myrtle awaited her arrival with great eagerness and, indeed, ran out into the snow to greet her shod only in satin slippers. The sisters embraced and all was forgiven between them. They went directly to the sick chamber where the earl lay, gray faced, upon his downy pillow.

"Father?" Helena placed her cool hand on his cheek. Hearing his beloved daughter's voice, the ancient man awoke with a rejuvenated spirit. With both his devoted girls to care for him, the earl recovered his health and lived for many years yet.

Helena told her father of her dream to convert their mansion into a new St. Jerome's Home for Foundlings, and he bestowed the house upon her with joy. He soon became known as Granpapa to all the orphans and sat by the fire each evening, telling stories to an enchanted audience.

Captain Brigand and his men never again needed to rob a train. They became upright citizens who taught the orphans riding, gymnasium, and cooking. Lady Myrtle became the instructor of penmanship and manners, though shortly she was wed with Joseph and began a family, which bloomed to nine children. Only occasionally was she heard to use cross words.

Elizabeth, the maid, was wed with Harry (the undergroom being sacked for drinking spirits).

Helena was wed with Tom, but she never had to cook, for he became a master chef of worldwide fame.

Helena dedicated herself to teaching children, her greatest desire being that each should discover what he (or she) wished to pursue as a life's work and not be forced to toil hopelessly for poor wages or merciless employers. That each should be curious and read books and be brave enough to follow his (or her) dream.

THE END

I have grown so accustomed to Mr. Goodhand's nightly readings that I shall miss them when we move.

"A meeting of the Ladies Reading Circle will take place on Sunday afternoon at the home of Mrs. Watson. All ladies are welcome. Refreshments will be served.

"You'd think they'd run out of books, wouldn't you?" asked Mr. Goodhand.

"Shall we go this time, Mable?" said Viola. "I think I'm ready to make some friends in Sellerton."

I realized that I had never told her what the Ladies Reading Circle truly was.

"I think that's a grand idea," I said.

Perhaps I would prepare her. Perhaps not.

ACKNOWLEDGMENTS

I was lucky to find two of my grandmother's diaries in the attic of her house, one hundred years after she had written them. Her days were as dull as dirty windows, but I read about them with a thrill of inspiration. The flavour of her penciled notes – though certainly not the content – formed the beginning of *Mable Riley*.

I would like to thank the following people for helping this book come to life: Jamie Michalak, my editor, for asking me to add instead of cut; Kathy Lowinger, for loving the manuscript; Martha Slaughter, for kitchen table brainstorming; Ethan Ellenberg, my agent, for his faith; Dr. Matt Nebel, for his veterinary guidance; Sara Reynolds, for always listening; my writing mates, Michele Spirn, Julia Noonan, Roxane Orgill, and Ellen Dreyer, for their treasured opinions; Alissa Heyman, for thoughtful early input; Sally Hill and the other librarians at the Stratford Public Library; Elaine Cook, caretaker of the Brocksden country schoolhouse for letting me peek inside, off-season; the archivists in the Perth County Archives; and of course, my family, Tom, Hannah, and Nell.